E. A. BAGBY

The Journey

The Feigned Moon of Entiria Epic Serial, Episode One

To my sons Aidan and Austin for all of their hard work and patience and for believing in me how I believe in them.

1

Many Days

Salihandron's gaping stone mouth filled my sight as I approached, a black void on a night with no bright moons.

According to ancient lore, the deity's throat was the Demon's Hold and the Spirit Passage. Its persistent exhale was the Great Breath, a physical manifestation of the god's essence. The wind howled from that rocky hole, whipping my clothes and hair and forcing me to lean forwards on the grassy land to stay stable.

Within my clutched fingers was a golden machine, the Progenitor of Understanding, as I'd come to think of it, or the glitch, a device that should never have been. Its presence had undermined me as a leader in our tribe, and I'd be happy if that were all it would do. It could ruin everything for me.

I raised my fist to throw the item into the god's mouth and rid myself of the curse.

But I stalled.

The few who knew of the machine would hate what I was about to do.

I dropped my hand and opened my palm. The singular item's pinprick-sized blue light glowed, highlighting features reminiscent of intertwining golden leaves and open petals. Such beauty.

The thoughts and words it possessed could reveal the past and change the future. Humanity might celebrate its arrival forever if I allowed it, if I shared it. A longing stabbed my chest.

Suppose I fed it to the god. Yes, the divinity would swallow it, and my problems could have vanished. But I would deprive everyone of the knowledge that would have helped them see the World as it truly was.

How could a device originally designed to do one thing—record our voices—be the World's most destructive power?

* * *

Many days before . . .

I stepped out of the back stairs onto the earthen berm, our underground home beneath my feet, aluminum spear in hand. Sunlight pressed on my face, animal calls filled the air, and the summer forest's fragrant breeze drifted past, relaxing my body.

My head still pounded from my hours of studying with Mother, who was working me hard to be the Deoan tribe's honored Lead Storyteller.

The Council of Seven Elders planned to declare a successor for when my mother retired from the role, even though that should be years away. A hundred experienced Storytellers clamored to be next in line, yet somehow, my parents expected me, their son, to be selected by the shamans.

Thankfully, my parents also depended on me for hunting, giving me a reprieve from the endless preparations. And I'd grown fast at achieving a kill, which allowed me a few extra moments to myself during the hunt.

I followed the trail through dense underbrush and small trees, passing a large square hole in the ground, our home's courtyard below, where Father was trimming a long-leaf arachea plant. Walking on the balls of my feet, I crouched so he wouldn't see me and take up this free time with chatter, then scuttled down an embankment, hopped over a seasonal stream, and scrambled up a hill with plenty of roots as handholds.

The hilltop granted me the highest ground in the Old Neighborhood and my favorite view. The ocean of tree canopies shrouding the Deo Commons and the North and East Neighborhoods stopped my breath, as always.

The point of my spear followed the landscape, tracing a line far north, past that unvaried sea of dark green. The Deo ended where a different forest began, with much taller trees growing over uneven, undulating terrain. Why was there so little speculation about who or what might live there? It was as if no one cared.

Maybe Cleo and I should visit that land when my studying ended, which would be soon. The Equis Ceremony, where the shamans would decide my fate, was only weeks away.

Patience.

Right then, Cleo and my other friends might have been at our favorite gathering place in the commons under the thick canopy before me, bantering and sharing stories, enjoying the *fenha*, the place's positivity.

An ache formed in my chest, a longing that pulled at me. The studying had kept me from my friends, from Cleo, for months— if it weren't for the promise of so many benefits if the council chose me, I would've been there right now.

A breeze played on the treetops below, swaying the branches

like fingers calling me forwards.

Our meeting spot was only a half-hour stroll from where I stood.

Using my spear as a walking stick, I shuffled down an embankment and along rough game trails, hopping over the Deo Stream. From there, I meandered among the smooth umber trunks of the Deo trees on the commons' perfectly flat carpet of moss.

Having been away from the meeting spot for so long made me meander aimlessly for a moment. But I found my way. Nothing in the commons interrupted sight lines except the innumerable tree trunks, giving me views of hundreds of feet in some directions.

A distant sight added a bounce to my step. Cleo's copper-gold Deoan cabin vehicle, or cab, rested on its parking skis among the trees' natural colonnades.

Every cab was simply a floating hull with wings. Hers looked like a metal egg with long strings of silvery wing-facets arranged like leaves on vines sprouting from the top of the hull. A ring of windowpanes separated by curved muntins wrapped the circumference—a pretty cab, for certain—bright, confident, and understated. Perfectly her.

Cleo's feet peeked out from beyond a familiar oversized tree.

My heart raced. This was what I'd really hoped for: Cleo by herself.

I rounded the tree, and she turned with a smile and a gleam in her wide, dreamy eyes. "Giels! Where have you been?"

"Where've *you* been?"

We laughed. It often felt like we thought the same things. A huge grin spread across my face, knowing we were still in sync after so long, as best friends ought to be.

A tan full-body wrap with lines of red and blue along the sides hugged Cleo. A slighter, younger version of her must have clung to my memories because her elegant, mature figure struck me.

She pushed herself up and pulled her straight, dark brown hair into a tail, revealing a face a shade lighter than the sepia tree she leaned against—a true Deoan, like me. Her hand patted the ground beside her.

Placing my hunting spear against the tree, I stretched out on the bright green moss. We embraced, filling me with a calm I hadn't had in a while.

"How are things with Mother, Giels?" she said, mocking my mother's overly formal tone and pronunciation of my name, *Gee-ells*, instead of *Gee-uhls*, as everyone else said.

I rolled my eyes, running a hand through my short, probably messy, hair. "She's been training me for fourteen hours a day for the damn Equis. Hunting is my only escape—that and sleep. The council is meeting tonight, and we're out of meat, so here I am." I tapped my spear.

"Since when are people allowed to hunt in the commons?" she asked.

"We're not. But . . ."

During the past four months, while memorizing the ancient one-and-a-half-hour story *The Sun and Moons* with my mother, I'd occasionally visited Cleo's neighborhood to hunt. I'd also dropped by her home. Every time, her mother or father would tell me she'd left for the day. "You're never home. Your parents were supposed to ask you to come see me."

She crossed her arms and lifted her button chin. "Honestly, I didn't want to disturb your studies," she said, still with a haughty tone.

"That's what I want . . . need."

She offered her water skin, simply decorated with an array of angled blue lines. "Your mother must be proud to pass the title onto her son," she said, her voice returning to normal. "Knowing her, she'd hate people coming by, distracting you."

I took a sip of water and handed the skin back. "I'm numb. It's her perfectionism. We'll repeat a single sentence for an hour until I have every intonation of every syllable just how it's *supposed* to be. It's why I need a distraction. Making it worse, Elder Sparus is at it again, always coming by and lecturing. Such an idiot."

"Is he still preaching about evil in the Rambles swamps?"

"No, I haven't been there in months. Now he's saying *we're* surrounded by evil."

She blinked, confused. "Who?"

"You know—you, me, Erikal, Meritus. I think he mentioned Meritus's shy friend Alana, even. Something about a nefarious otherworldly being's influence."

Cleo turned away and spat out a sip of water. She gave me a soft push with her shoulder. "The Sun! An idiot *and* a loon. Almost can't believe he's a shaman." Her features turned crooked and evil, though somehow still cute. "I am Elder Sparus's tortured imagination!"

I chuckled. "He was especially worked up this morning, rushing in to see Father about something 'unspeakable,' which made me wonder how he would speak about it. You should come over, seriously. You're right, my mother hates distractions, but she specifically asked about *you*."

"Oh? Okay, sure. I've just been very busy."

"'Busy?' So, where *have* you been?"

"Here, sometimes. But also, Erikal's workshop."

Erikal? What does she need from him? They'd never spent time alone that I knew of.

He was one of my closest friends, but Meritus, his best friend, often visited his workshop to seek help with the computer. Although each home had a computer, not everyone understood the computer-spirit well enough to design complex machines. Erikal had tremendous skill, which must have been why she'd been going to him. "Was he helping you or something?"

"Just my cab. The wings are now forward of the fulcrum, compensating for the wingplate's limited angles. I would have made it that way originally if I knew it was possible." She stared at me, eyes twinkling.

I shrugged, not understanding half of what she'd said. "And?"

"Sorry," she said. "I mean *it's faster now*. I've been around someone fixated on cabs. I think I'm starting to talk like him." She rolled her eyes.

Jealousy over her working a bunch with Erikal hit like a punch. "Didn't know you were *that* interested in cabs."

"It's so exciting," she said. "The diagrams on Erikal's computer have more cab design options than my family's for some reason. And, actually, Meritus and I helped Erikal assemble a fantastic new cab he's designed, too."

My jealousy worsened to a sinking feeling in my heart until her eyes met mine. She looked down and plucked a lone blade of grass that peeked through the moss. "Maybe we can take a ride in mine. You'll see how nice it is."

Warmth gathered in my stomach. We'd need to sit very close in a small cab like hers.

I nodded. "I was just thinking it's about time we go outside the Deo—put all that travel training to use."

"Definitely. Actually, I'm glad you came by. I was hoping to talk to you about a trip."

I found myself stealing a glance at her full lips, watching her slightly open mouth, reminding me that it had once touched mine, something youths seldom did except those who planned to marry. Her attempted kiss had shocked me and, having been younger then, I'd foolishly run away.

Because we were close, lifelong friends, I had always stopped myself from making a similarly bold move. But my best friend had grown beautiful to me over the years, even more so since I'd last seen her, making contradictory feelings about friendship and passion swirl in my head and chest. With her lips red like a rare night flower, a sudden surge of desire overcame me, and I wanted to make the kiss happen.

Placing one hand on the ground behind her, I allowed my arm to make the gentlest contact with her back. She was less subtle. Weaving her hand between my arm and torso, she leaned against me.

I pulled in a breath of contentment. We'd been apart too long.

She and I hadn't outright decided to marry, but the time for that discussion grew ever more pressing. We were well within marrying age. Our close families hinted continuously at it. We'd been friends our entire lives. We never bored each other and could talk for hours.

It all seemed so obvious. Perfect, even.

Lost in my thoughts, I leaned in close, our faces now only a hand-length apart. We smiled.

I moved closer. A first kiss was traditional before asking to marry.

From far off on my left, a deep voice called, "Giels!"

My entire body slumped.

Erikal. Really?

"Speaking of the man," Cleo said, pushing herself up to see

past me. A contented sigh escaped her.

Man? I still thought of us as boys and girls. And why had she sighed like that?

"Look who's emerged, finally," Erikal said, looking at me. "Suppose I can give you this now."

He hurried towards us with his broad shoulders and self-assured manner. In that moment, his focused, thoughtful eyes, set within the lighter, beige skin of a more northern tribe, had an almost mischievous gleam. I wished he hadn't come—not right now—but his intense stare commanded my attention, as it usually did to those around him.

Erikal shot Cleo a smile reeking of a special bond between them. It made me wince. He rarely smiled.

Glancing back at me, he returned to his serious expression and tossed a small device.

"The recorder," he said as I caught it. "Remember? It was *your* idea."

Cleo leaned in to take a look.

The articulated copper-gold, finger-length object—cylindrical and covered mainly in foil-thin golden petals like an imaginary swamp flower about to bloom—teetered in my hand. Decorative knots covered exposed portions of the cylinder. I ran my fingers along the delicate petal edges. The item possessed a haunting beauty.

"Did you say '*recorder*'?" I asked.

He nodded. "A voice recorder."

My mouth gaped, and my eyes ran all over its small parts.

We had the word *recorder* in our language, but I doubted many knew it, and the word seemed wrapped in awe and magic. I hadn't heard it more than a few times in my life, in fact, despite training as a storyteller. It never appeared in our canon stories, only offhand in informal legends, like taboo whispers, as though such devices had been familiar to humanity long ago, and only the word survived as a remnant, like an impression of blurred childhood memory or the suppressed recollection of an agonizing past.

I glanced at Erikal, whose stare returned confident pride, as it often did.

Cleo pinched the machine from my palm and rotated it in the dappled Sunlight. Its golden details shimmered.

How had he made something so unusual?

The computer-spirit was the greatest of all the mechanical spirits because it helped us design everything. It almost seemed like a creator-god, except that gods exerted their influence from afar through meditation or weather—excluding Salihandron, the death-escort, of course. But having never paid much attention to computers, for all I knew, they would help anyone make a recorder, but only Erikal had thought to try.

"This was your idea?" Cleo said to me.

"Yeah, I suppose. I don't know. Months ago, Erikal mentioned he worked out schematics for recording sound. I wanted to hear myself reciting lore."

I'd meant it as a joke, not believing a device to do that was possible.

"Honestly, wasn't easy," Erikal said, sticking out his hand.

Cleo passed him the machine.

"The recordings never go away, so I won't add anything. But I'll show you how it works," he said with a tone like he was about to teach a younger crowd.

Without actually touching the two buttons, he demonstrated various ways to use them—quickly pressing a button did one thing, pushing them both for a couple of seconds did another, and so on.

"Enjoy," he added. He spun around without a goodbye, walking towards a vehicle in the distance. I could see only parts of it through all the tree trunks, but its hull's copper-and-chromadium panelling had an unusual recursive-but-naturalistic pattern, like something grown, a slightly more florid version of a swamp-crab's shell. Another impressive design, even for Erikal.

"Is that your new ship?" I called after him.

He turned. "Right. You haven't seen it, which reminds me . . ." He walked back. "Don't know if Cleo told you, but we're planning an adventure with Alana and Meritus—and you, if you want."

If we weren't going somewhere alone, I wanted to be sure I'd be riding in Cleo's cab the entire time. "I'll ride with you," I said to her.

She blinked as if surprised. "We're only taking Erikal's."

The largest cabs fit a cramped four. Putting aside the improbability of Erikal's new ship fitting all of us, I asked, "When?"

"One week from today," Erikal said.

An ironic laugh escaped me. He'd certainly made a joke, but his characteristically thoughtful eyes remained.

"That'll make the trip during the public Equis rehearsal," I said. "You remember I'm performing, right? Just wait a few—"

"Sorry," Erikal interrupted, waving a hand. "That's when the moons will be brightest. We might be driving for three days, including at night. It'll be months before the night is as bright again."

Three full days? That's farther than most in our tribe had gone. He wasn't serious, was he? "Then I can't go."

"You can make your own choices, Giels," he said with the

relaxed, overconfident tone of someone a decade older than his nineteen years.

He knew I couldn't take chances with becoming the Lead Storyteller, making his dismissive, waxing-shamanistic advice a taunt. Too much depended on the title. Most people's work amounted to tending to their gardens and creating objects and tools for their families with computers, while I'd only recite lore, with everything else handed to me, if I so desired.

It almost seemed Erikal, my good friend, didn't care if I joined him.

He gave his temple a light smack. "How'd I forget? Have the recorder recite back to you from the very beginning. There's a message. You'll want to listen to it. Trust me."

He threw a quick palm up in an aloof, Erikal-style wave goodbye and smiled at Cleo—again.

"I'll be there tomorrow," she responded.

My head swiveled through their interaction. Then he was off, winding his way between the trees before I could ask him about his message.

His ship lifted from the mossy ground and floated soundlessly out of sight.

"I was about to tell you about the trip before Erikal came by," Cleo said. "Come with us."

I folded my arms across my chest. "You haven't visited me so I could practice. Now you want me to leave the Deo during my public rehearsal?"

"What can I do? Erikal is very eager."

"So? When's he not eager?"

She shrugged. "True. But imagine how fun it'll be. Erikal's cab is fantastic and huge, and *fast*!"

Another pang hit my stomach. More than one girl, including

Cleo, had told me I was handsome. And many, especially Cleo, loved my penchant for vocabulary and memorizing ancient stories. I wouldn't have cared how impressed she seemed with Erikal or all the time they'd spent together if it weren't for his confidence, firm muscles, cleverness with the computer, ability to make the best vehicles, half a head above me in height, and exotic looks.

I rubbed my face out of irritation.

Cleo had once, long ago, confided that her parents had suggested Erikal as a possible husband. Supposedly, not until I recited the forty-five-minute story *Sahra's Bane* in front of them a few years back did they prefer me.

"Your mother and father will probably be at the rehearsal," I said, knowing shamans sought parental approval before officiating a marriage.

She rolled her eyes. "Who cares about my parents? You're overthinking again. It sounds like you're overworking yourself. With your talent, this should be easy. I'm sure the council pretends to care about the rehearsal to make it appear more serious. The real Equis is not for, what, another three weeks? You'll be Lead Storyteller regardless."

She was pushing hard, but I shook my head. Even if the rehearsal didn't matter much for my readiness, my parents and the council certainly wouldn't see it that way. The elders weren't a lenient group and had plenty of other candidates.

"With Erikal's cab," she added, "faraway places won't be limited to just talk in your lore. We can actually *go* to Mount Saris, Tulur mesa, Bael lands, the cave, the Great River."

I furrowed my brow and shifted away from her. *Just talk in my lore?*

Cleo rested her fingers on my palm, where the recorder still sat. An electrical sensation ran up my arm, pulling me back to her.

"It's beautiful," she said, "like a golden bromeliad."

"Erikal didn't show you this when you visited all those times?" I asked.

"No."

"Alright. Let's give it a try." At least we'd be able to experience *this* together. I pressed the button as Erikal had instructed, and a tiny blue light appeared on its side. I put it close to my mouth. "Hello, recorder. Capture my voice."

I pressed the other button.

"Hello, recorder. Capture my voice," it repeated as clearly as a person.

"That's absolutely amazing," Cleo said.

"Do I sound that funny?"

"It sounds like you. Tell it more."

"You should say something," I said, pressing the record button again.

"But your voice is lovely, Giels. Talk about the Deo. Maybe we can even have the recorder recite it to people when we go on our trip, and they can learn about us."

"Clever idea," I said. And it seemed a perfect opportunity to remind Cleo of my family's status. "Many things, like the Deo trees and the Deo tribe itself, are named after my surname, Deo. You see, my ancestors founded our tribe."

That grabbed her attention. She slapped my arm, her large eyes rolling. "Braggart."

"*You* told me to tell it about the Deo."

She scrunched her nose. "Have it recite from the start to hear Erikal's message."

"No doubt it's a belated birthday message telling me this is my gift." I waved the recorder. "He missed my eighteenth, remember? Probably to make that giant cab." I clicked the back button twice to go to the beginning, and the machine's light blinked.

But it repeated my words, "Hello, recorder. Capture—"

I stopped the device. "Didn't Erikal say the blinking means it's at the start?" I tried several more times to hear his message with the same result. "It's malfunctioning." Perhaps the device wasn't so great, after all. "He changed your cab. Are you sure *that* is still safe?"

She screwed up her face.

A bright reflection caught my eye. Some distance away, three cabs clad in their shining metal weaved towards us through the trees. Meritus was in the lead. No one had raced cabs before he'd come up with the idea—at least, not in our lifetimes.

Cleo shook her head. "I'm surprised Meritus hasn't crashed, racing here like that every evening."

Evening?

Through the canopy, the Sun edged close to the horizon. Surprised by how much time had passed, I jumped up. My mother would have expected me back already. "I need to go. Meritus will try to keep me here." I shoved the recorder into my pocket. "Talk to Erikal about the device. See if it's malfunctioning. Come visit me after," I added, mainly to give her a reason to come over. "I could honestly use some encouragement, Cleo. It's tough, what I'm going through, and *everything* hinges on the coming weeks."

"I'll come if I can. We're preparing for the journey. Tweaking Erikal's cab has been a lot."

My head burned, suddenly.

She'd miss my rehearsal to go off with him without me unless

I shirked my responsibilities.

"Okay. Fine. Have fun," I said, stomping away to hide my searing face.

2

NO

"What?!" My father let out a full belly laugh. "Did you say 'miss the rehearsal'?"

When I'd approached my home after leaving Cleo, his backside had greeted me while he knelt in the garden. He hadn't even bothered to turn around before laughing at me.

My father, the Lead Elder of the Deo—the tribe's most important role—had been plowing long rows of seed furrows. His white shaman's robe, taut because of his position, revealed a body much wider than the one I remembered from childhood.

"Well, Father, it's just that—"

"'Well, Father, it's just that,'" he copied in his deep, loud voice. I heard the scowl that must have been on his face. Did he think himself funny? "It's just that," he added, "it's just that I might need to go talk to the council right now and tell them you're not interested in being Lead Storyteller."

"Father, that's not—"

"Do you see my bulbs?" The seemingly lighthearted question boomed out. His head pivoted to the right.

"They're on your left," I said, "by your feet."

"Oh, yes, right. Thank you, Giels." His tone softened. As he often did, he went from heated to mild with complete sincerity and without blinking an eye. I could never parse whether he had amazing emotional control or a sort of emotional chaos.

Father picked up the flower bulbs, turned his soil-smudged face to me, and deactivated his do-it-all, a vertical cylindrical device that did not do it all—just basic work like hammering, cutting, and digging. The machine casually floated out of his way.

"Why are you planting flowers?" I asked, more to defuse the tension than out of any interest.

"We've plenty of vegetables and, well, thought it was time to finally . . . uh, where'd I put them now?" His head spun around, locating where he had just moved the bowl.

"Father," I said, taking advantage of the calm moment and deepening my voice to sound confident, "why do I need to be at the rehearsal? You know hardly anyone will be there. I'll be ready without it."

He placed one of the bulbs in the small trench. "It's tradition. And you know the council insists you be there or they'll disqualify you. Anyhow, they're busy at the actual Equis; it's the practice where they'll observe you more. What in the world between the earth and sky is so important to miss it?"

"I need a break," I said, throwing out my arms. "I've gone through all that travel training, yet I've never left the Deo, except that fiasco with the Talis envoy, and that was years ago. Erikal says the moons will be extra bright next week, and he's waiting for that to go. He asked me to join."

"Emba and Hola will both be full in the sky—and, come to think of it, Dorel, too." He nodded. "Yes, starting a couple nights before the Equis rehearsal. Erikal, huh? He's driving at night?"

I shrugged. "Apparently."

"I haven't heard about this. Where's he planning to go?"

"Don't know," I said. "Somewhere outside the Deo. He wants to try out his new cab."

"Oh, yes. I've heard about this vehicle. Your friend Meritus told Elder Sparus about it in great detail yesterday. A cab that can seat five or more, I believe, no? Makes even a shaman wonder how Erikal does it."

I rolled my eyes. Did our tribe's most influential spiritual guide not understand how the computer worked? Or had he not noticed Erikal's obvious talent with it? Sometimes I wondered how he became a shaman, let alone the lead shaman.

He put down his gloves. "I must insist you not go."

I knew he would say that, but I needed to persist. Occasionally, he gave in to me. I channeled what Cleo had said, hoping Father would see reason. "I've hardly left the house for four months. It's just a *practice* Equis."

He sighed, scratching his head. "It's, well, not just the rehearsal, although that's critical. It's something the council is discussing. I— I can't explain right now. You need to trust me."

There he goes again, keeping his shamanistic wisdom from me, asking me to trust him without him trusting me. "What is it? Why can't you explain?"

"Hopefully, I can soon. And, hopefully, it's nothing important. Just . . . don't take a journey in Erikal's new vehicle for now. Understand? We have questions about, well . . . let's just say his highly inspired designs of late. And please say nothing about this. I don't want to bother Erikal without good cause."

"'Don't want to bother Erikal'?" I said. "What about me? And what's wrong with his designs? He's good at it. 'The spirit inspires him,' as *you'd* say."

My father only stared at me. I knew he would talk no more about it.

Erikal's vehicle was probably why Elder Sparus had been coming by to hassle me about evil spirits haunting my friends. Typical. Anything even mildly different unnerved that elder.

My face grew hot. I covered it with my hands, and a growl escaped me.

"Be patient, Giels. After the Equis, maybe I can have one of the other council elders lend you their nice, big cab, and you can go on a journey somewhere with Cleo."

With Cleo. At times, he knew how to get to me. He'd managed to say the one thing that would defuse my frustration, especially considering we had no cab of our own. I tried holding back a smile, but he caught on to it. His mouth stretched into a huge grin.

"Sure, whatever," I said, and turned before my smile materialized, walking one of the garden's fieldstone paths to the earthen berm covering our home.

Father whistled a tune that followed me as I stepped into the underground concrete-and-limestone entry corridor. The glass door within slid up between hewn stones and slid back after I passed, muting his song.

I stopped at the computer, something relegated to a nook in the entry passage. We rarely used it, letting other families provide us with the things we needed, a benefit of my father being the Lead Elder and my mother the Lead Storyteller.

Excited for my attention, the machine activated its dark titanium screen with moving copper-gold etchings of machine-part schematics.

The computer resembled a kitchen floor cabinet, except that it had an angled metallic display screen instead of a counter. Next to the computer was the producer, a metal box with a funnel on top—we dropped the often-rare raw materials in, and the completed component appeared inside.

I bowed slightly out of respect for the computer-spirit that dwelled within. My only interest in computers was to wonder occasionally how the deep etchings moved within the solid metal panel. But the idea of creating another recorder made me curious.

After running my thumb along the screen's right-hand side to cycle through line diagrams of basic typologies—a one-seater cab for vehicles, a door for home architecture, a cup washer for kitchen items, a cap for clothes, and so on—I stopped. Which typology would a recorder be? I honestly had no idea. I couldn't even get past the first step in making one.

It occurred to me that I'd left the one in my pocket recording. Toying with it, I opened the golden petals around its circumference a tiny bit, which Erikal had said increased its volume.

I had it go back to somewhere near the beginning of my conversation with my father. "WHAT IN THE WORLD—" His voice boomed through the home. Panicked, I stopped and pocketed the device.

"Danis?" my mother called from somewhere, her strong, articulate voice full of concern. "Why are you yelling?"

If my father and Elder Sparus were worried about Erikal's computer usage, I thought it better not to share the recorder he'd made just yet. Thinking quickly, I called back, "It's just me . . . practicing my voice projection."

"You are starting to sound like your father."

My father didn't want me to miss the rehearsal or go with Erikal, but if one parent agreed with me, usually the other would.

I took in a deep breath, then let it out. I needed to be calm and seem responsible when I asked Mother.

I found her sitting on a pillow in the main living area next to the glass wall surrounding the open-air courtyard. She held her back straight, hands in her lap, head high, her persistent look of important seriousness on her thin, somewhat-youthful face. Her hand ran over her torso, straightening or brushing off her sleeveless white blouse, which had several horizontal blue lines around the chest. She pulled in a lungful of air through her nose and glared at me.

I affected my most charming smile.

Mother's brow furrowed. "I see you have nothing after all that time. How is that possible? The elders will be here soon, expecting meat."

My smile dropped. I glanced at my empty hands, which should have been carrying a kill.

She shook her head. "You go away for hours when there is still so much studying to do. It is up to you to maintain the line of shamans and Lead Storytellers on your father's side. Are you now ready?"

She was mad. That was more pressure than usual.

I examined my trimmed fingernails, giving myself a moment of reprieve. Probably not a good time to ask about missing the Equis rehearsal.

The magical Billencen Device, a family heirloom with an unknown purpose, which was resting on a nearby oaken counter, tapped at random intervals. Its chromadium rod's center point balanced on a pewter pyramid, bobbing around and sometimes hitting the counter with its ends. Generation upon generation had heard the magic device's quiet ticking, which now only served to remind me that my mother awaited a response.

I wouldn't complain to her. At my age, I understood the future I'd always envisioned was tied to the Lead Storyteller title and its benefits.

Sitting on a pillow beside her, I looked her in the eye and nodded to signal my readiness. I figured her mood should improve after we rehearsed a bit, and I could then ask about missing the practice Equis.

"Good," she said. "As I was saying before you went . . . hunting, it is 'Wander over paths did Karranae, passing under Sun's light through clouds grey.' Not '. . . passing *in* Sun's light . . .' as you and your friends might say. That changes the meaning and cadence."

"I know, but doesn't it make more sense with 'in'? We walk *in* the Sun's light, not *under* it."

Why did I just say that to her? I braced for the lecture she'd given me many times, always in the exact same wording.

She pulled in a deep breath. "The stories are us. They are our past, our history. They are who we are as a tribe and the one constant in the World. If you or I change a story out of selfish or careless reasons, it will be lost to your children and their children and on until the end of time. If we cannot get this perfectly correct, then we have failed the World."

The last sentence was new. *Fail the World?* How did I make her that mad?

Or maybe it was as Cleo had said: People were trying to make my recitation seem way more important than it was.

But I wouldn't challenge the point. Not now. She'd just grow more insistent.

I exhaled a slow breath. Whether or not Mother was right about me possibly failing the World, I wouldn't ask her about missing the Equis rehearsal.

* * *

Later that evening, we stopped rehearsing in anticipation of the shamans arriving for the Council of Seven Elders' meeting. I left my mother to throw myself into bed before any shamans arrived, complaining that there were no meat dishes.

"Young Deo," Elder Sparus said from my right before I could exit the living area.

My body spasmed at the unexpected sardonic voice.

Sparus had called me from the entry corridor, coming in without announcing himself, as usual. He stood like a statue. As they always did, his eyes twinkled with a look that suggested he knew more than he would let on.

The thin, middle-aged man held his arms across his chest, each hand tucked into the sleeve of the other. "You appear rushed."

"I was just going to find game before your meeting. Something fast to cook." I couldn't lie to an elder, which meant I was now committed to another hunt. "Dusk raptor. You know, they're out at this time."

"Ah, yes," the elder said, "the perils of young adulthood. Caught between frivolity and responsibilities. How are our studies?"

I always hated it when he said *our* when he meant *your*.

"I'm close to ready." I smiled. The elders would decide my fate as Lead Storyteller not just by scrutinizing me during my Equis performance, but always. I straightened to appear responsible.

"You seem as tense as the game you'll be hunting," he said.

An embarrassed scoff escaped me. The elder had a way of exposing one's foibles. I placed my hands behind my back to appear more casual.

The elder raised a skeptical eyebrow, suggesting I looked even more wooden.

"You honor us early, Elder Sparus," I said to regain myself.

"Yes. And seeing you here reminds me that I wanted to bring up some unusual happenings at our meeting." The way he stared at me made me feel he was accusing me of the unusual happenings, whatever they were. Was this about Erikal's computer usage, as my father had talked about, and did he think I'd snitch about it? Lying to elders might have been forbidden, but there was no rule against keeping my mouth shut, so I'd say nothing. He could just go talk with Erikal.

He held his gaze as though expecting a response.

"I see," he said, as if my awkward hesitation and beads of sweat were the response he waited for. "Young Giels," he added, "have you noticed how there is a limit to what gods allow, what the computer is capable of, and what the Council of Seven Elders agrees to?"

I shrugged. "Yes . . . I suppose. Haven't thought about it too much."

"Precisely. It all happens smoothly. It can make it seem as though everything is the way it should be. Just because you feel all goes as expected, it doesn't mean that all you do is right."

I winced despite trying to seem respectful. "Am I doing something wrong?"

"You tell me."

My face turned hot. Why was he lecturing me about vague nonsense when I already had enough to worry about?

Sparus strolled to the entry closet, opened its door, and handed me an aluminum spear from within. "Good luck."

3

If You Leave

After being denied a chance to join my friends on their upcoming trip, I went to bed each night hoping Cleo would come see me the next day. I imagined her folded in my arms, imploring my mother to allow me to join her. My mother would say no, and Cleo, taken by sudden passion, would promise to marry me after the Equis and go on our own journey.

She did not.

The best I could do was focus intently on my recitation. After the council anointed me as the next Lead Storyteller, Erikal's adventure would be a single brief memory, fading compared to the string of new memories Cleo and I would create.

Two days before the rehearsal, I'd almost perfected the correct inflections for stanza one-hundred forty-seven, line two of *The Sun and Moons* when the sound of our house's entry door sliding up stopped me mid-sentence.

Cleo called my name. My back straightened immediately.

"Come in, Cleo!" Mother shouted.

My friend emerged from the entrance passage in a knee-length dress covered in colorful, curving geometric patterns—

her design, certainly. Cleo liked experimenting with fabrics and their prints. A braid, resting on one breast, kept her hair out of her face, and she wore sandals with straps that crisscrossed her calves. She had dressed nicely, which was customary when visiting, but she looked particularly fresh and perfect that day. She looked so good, in fact, it made me uncomfortable, like I was ordinary by comparison.

Cleo bowed a little, something expected because of my mother's title. "May I talk to Giels a moment, Lead Storyteller Bria Deo?"

"Yes, Cleo, of course," Mother said, with her crystal-clear articulate voice. "We can take a break. Would you want to stay? It will only take me a moment to prepare a lunch."

"No, thank you. I'll not be here long."

The formalities over with, my mother nodded and moved around the corner of the court's glass wall.

I jumped up. "I'm so happy you came by. I'm exhausted, and the elders—"

"Shhh," she said. "Let's go to your room."

My room? My palms grew sweaty. She hadn't been in my room for ages.

She grabbed one of my clammy hands and pulled me to the bedroom. The brushed-chrome door slid shut behind us.

Perhaps she wants to kiss. She's going away on an adventure, which I need to miss because of one of the most important events of my life, one of the most important events of the Deo. Perhaps she even wanted to do more than kiss.

My excitement must have beamed on my face. She glanced at me, almost a double-take, before sitting on my bed.

I joined her, wrapping an arm around her waist and leaning against my bedroom's cool ashlar wall. She looked down at my arm and, sitting back with me, she put her palm on my other hand. Her eyes stared into mine.

Is she waiting for me?

My eyelids drooped slightly, and I felt my face move towards hers.

She shook her head a fraction and blinked. "Do you have your recorder?"

I stopped. "Recorder?"

"Yes. I talked with Erikal."

My heart sank. Erikal's message? I'd forgotten about it. "That's why you came by? I haven't seen you for an entire week."

"I know. Sorry. Told you we'd be busy preparing for the journey."

"So, it's malfunctioning?"

"No, Erikal insists there's something in there. At the beginning."

I pulled away from her, sitting straight. "We already tried."

"Let me try again." She held out her palm.

It happened to be in my pocket. Confused, I pulled out the device. She plucked it from me.

"Erikal wanted us to listen to it before you recorded anything," she said.

"I'd remember if he said that. He didn't."

"I didn't think so, but he said that's what he wanted. Actually, Meritus and Alana heard his recording before Erikal gave it to you, but they refused to tell me about it. They said listening is much, much better."

"It's a birthday message, isn't it?"

She turned the device in her fingers. "No. They said it's the reason for the trip, and they think it'll convince you to go."

I scoffed. "Why would Erikal have recorded something to

convince me to go? I need no convincing. I already wish I could." Besides, if he really wanted me to go, he could have planned it so he and Cleo wouldn't have more time together without me. The thought made a dart of pain shoot to my forehead.

She pressed the button that made it go backwards in the recordings. The device's tiny blue light blinked. "Hello, recorder. Capture my—" it said with my voice. Cleo stopped it.

"See," I said, "there's nothing there. Erikal said the recordings never go away. I don't know what the others think they heard. He probably made two recorders or something."

She looked straight into my eyes. "No. I saw the diagrams for the recorder's design on Erikal's computer. They're odd—they don't allow replication of this device for some reason." She furrowed her brow and looked down. "One moment. I believe he said to..." Her thumb tapped one of the two buttons a number of times as if to a rhythm.

Nothing.

I rolled my eyes. "I told you—"

"Can you hear me?" the recorder said. It sounded like I imagined a pixie's voice would—high, somewhat screeching, and inhuman.

We both shot up. The device fell from Cleo's hand onto the fieldstone floor. It neither bounced nor slid from where it landed.

"This is what we've been waiting for," it continued. "From the ether, you have found me. We are of the other world. Return me through the passage."

There was silence, then it was me again. "Hello, recorder. Capture my voice."

Cleo looked at me, and I looked back at her, stunned.

Fearing the fall had damaged the recorder's delicate petals,

I quickly picked it up and stopped it. It remained in perfect condition.

"Sorry for dropping it," Cleo said.

"It seems fine. You haven't heard that?"

"The Sun, no."

I scoffed again. "Erikal's playing a prank. Maybe Meritus." Meritus loved pranking people, and Erikal often played along.

Cleo glanced down at the device. "It sounds nothing like them. The way he looked at me when I told him we hadn't listened to it, you wouldn't think it's a prank—like we've missed something mystical. Erikal's eyes were hazy, far away. Have you ever seen him look like that? I haven't."

"I can talk to my father—" I started, but I recalled what my father had said about Erikal's designs. I grimaced hard. "Never mind."

"Why 'never mind?'" she asked.

"When I mentioned the journey to him, he behaved strangely about Erikal. The council is suspicious of the things he's creating."

Her eyes widened. "Really?"

I nodded. "But he wouldn't tell me what that meant."

"Maybe they already know about the message."

"Not sure, but don't think so," I said. "I think Elder Sparus is just getting his robes in a bind over Erikal's creativity for no reason and getting the council worked up. I wasn't supposed to say anything about this. Promise you'll not tell Erikal."

"Promise."

"Why would Erikal think the message would encourage me to go?"

She tapped a finger on her lips. "Because this is the reason for the trip. He must have an idea of what to do. Actually, he mentioned we'll be bringing your recorder west."

I scoffed. "To the Lost Forest?" Nothing in the message would have made me think of that place. "What's he up to?"

"I don't know, honestly. He said he'll tell us later." Her eyes sparkled. "Isn't it exciting?" She shoved me with her shoulder. "Now you *have* to go."

My father, Elder Sparus, the recorder, the secrecy. "Seems more odd than exciting." Something occurred to me. "It *is* a prank." I chuckled.

"How?"

"Why would he give *me* the recorder if it's the entire reason he's going on an adventure?" I asked. "This is just his way of trying to get everyone excited for the trip."

She winced. "But why bother? We'd go anyway."

"You know Meritus," I said. "Probably his doing."

However, Cleo had a point. What would this prank achieve, and who would it make a joke of?

A new fear rushed in. The odd message would give Erikal a reason for his urgency, going the one time I couldn't join. Meritus seemed to have an interest in Alana, leaving Erikal and Cleo to spend time together in faraway romantic places. Yes, Erikal could be that clever.

He'd always talked about how pretty Cleo was. How close had they gotten while I studied at home with Mother?

I took a deep breath to calm myself. Could one adventure come between us, and would Erikal even do that?

Footsteps approached my door, followed by a knock.

"Giels," my mother said. "I have been waiting for you two to come out. Your gort is getting cold."

"One moment!" I said, and turned to Cleo, lowering my voice to a whisper. "I know you really want me to go. But we can go on our own adventure. My father said I could even use a shaman's cab. You know, once everything is set for me and before, well, before we . . ." *Before we marry*, I wanted to say.

Cleo stared deep into my eyes again. "Your father—I know how important it is you follow his wisdom. An adventure in one of the elders' cabs sounds nice, but if you want real adventure—and I know you do—this is it. It's what Erikal is doing tonight. I want that. You will be Lead Storyteller, which is amazing, but it will take so much of your time. Life will become routine, fixed, scheduled—and worse, you will need to represent the best character, as my parents and yours do all the time. It's exhausting. What about time for fun? Exploration? I want to marry someone spontaneous. I want excitement. And Erikal said this machine was your idea, one clever enough for him spend lots of time on. So, if you can't join this adventure, will you ever?"

My jaw dropped, and I recoiled as though I'd been slapped. She'd always made me feel that my storytelling prowess was one of my best qualities.

Did she worry I'd turn into my father and seldom go anywhere?

"Oh, Giels. I'm sorry," Cleo said. She must have seen the defeat I felt.

I swallowed. "This message is a joke. It means nothing."

Her face moved close to mine. Her sparkling eyes were so beautiful. My breaths deepened. A picture popped into my mind: Erikal and Cleo staring at some faraway landscape, his arm around her waist.

"Kiss me," I said. What I wanted had escaped my lips—not talk of cabs, or messages, or adventures. My heart pounded from surprise at my own request.

Cleo glanced around the room, a hint of a shocked smile on her face.

"Giels, please open this door," my mother's muffled voice said, now in a scolding tone. "I will need to come in out of fear something is wrong."

I wished the damn woman would just go away.

"Kiss? Your mother is right there!" Cleo said with a raspy whisper, pointing at the door.

"She probably believes we're kissing anyhow."

Cleo winced. "What? No," she said, her face growing flush. "If she's already suspicious, it's a terrible time to kiss. You know I love you, but I promise there's time to . . . kiss"—she grabbed my hand that held the recorder and raised it—"after *we* go on the adventure."

Cleo stood, slapped the door's open button, and slid past my mother.

Looking at Mother, I casually dropped the recorder in my pocket. She cocked her head to the side as though noticing my disappointment.

I stomped past her to my bowl of gort.

Cleo wanted the adventure Erikal offered. She wanted it so much that she'd suggested we might not have a life together if I didn't go, even though the trip was at the worst possible time.

What's gotten into you, Cleo?

* * *

In the deep dark of that night, I lay in my room, toying with the recorder. Despite myself, a tear fell from my eye. All of my toils, pent up, leaked into my mind, then flooded, making me realize I had worked too hard and too long to lose what I wanted.

I dressed in a fresh set of day clothes and paced my room.

Erikal may not have actually needed the recorder, nor wanted me to join them, but Cleo said something I could not let go of—that we'd kiss after *we* returned from the adventure.

After my parents deactivated the artificial lights and went to bed, I left my room. One of our courtyard's glass panels slid up to let me through.

My knees pressed hard against the flagstone in front of the fountain statue of Tohillocen, goddess of rain, caves, and inner thought, that stood in front of the court's one stone wall. Rarely had I sought her help. Rarely had I needed it.

Above me, the thousand stars glistened within the firmament as black as a cave.

The goddess statue's alabaster eyes, flecked with quartz, received enough starlight to shimmer, revealing the deity's distant stare.

"I want to go on his journey to the Lost Forest," I said to the statue. "Cleo *needs* me to. But I can't."

Even in the darkness, my family's beautiful courtyard and home filled me with its presence. If I didn't become a tribal leader, I'd lose the right to inherit all of it.

Cupping my hands, I caught cold water that poured from the statue's palms to the pool at her feet and splashed my forehead. I flinched. Its crispness shocked my nerves, cleansing my thoughts and opening my mind. But no epiphany came, no guidance on what I should do.

Time passed. The stars moved. My attention drifted to the recorder in my pocket and stayed there.

The harder I tried to shake the item from my thoughts, the stronger its imprint on my mind, as though the goddess forced it upon me. When fighting to stay focused on the journey brought me to the point of exhaustion, an idea hit like a punch.

The device is a glitch, a thing that should not be.

Had the goddess inspired this thought? I straightened and stared into the beautiful stone eyes. "I can sort out the device later. Cleo will go whether or not the message is real. I'm running out of time. I need to know if I should join her."

Before the goddess responded, movement to my left caught my attention. Light reflected on one of the courtyard's solid glass walls. I spun around.

A glowing orb, like faerie fire, floated about beyond one of the other transparent walls, inside my home. Were Elder Sparus's warnings of foul spirits true?

My heart raced.

I crept near to the glass to look inside, careful not to move too close and activate the clear sliding panel.

Four figures stood on the other side of the living area, by my bedroom's open door. One held a dim artificial lamp.

For a moment, the lamp lighted its holder's face—Erikal's. The three others with him became obvious. I released a tight breath and scoffed at myself for being spooked.

No glowing spirit haunted my home.

My friends walked towards where I crouched in the courtyard.

Damn. I turned to the goddess. "Tohillocen," I whispered, "if I don't go, will I lose Cleo? Give me something."

But nothing came to mind except the singular machine, the glitch, in my pocket.

4

An Otherwise Normal Morning

Not wanting my friends to find me crouched there in the courtyard, I stood. They approached. The courtyard's glass panel slid up between us.

Erikal shined his light on me. Cleo stood next to him, her face glowing in the reflection of my white shirt. "See. He wants to go," she said, her voice soft. Her face held the slightest of smiles, and her eyes glistened in the pale light. She'd come for me.

Tohillocen hadn't answered whether I should go with Cleo, risking my Lead Storyteller bid. Shamans would often say such silence during prayer was a command against rash decisions.

But I wouldn't heed the command.

Cleo stepped forwards, closing her fingers around my wrist.

I would create a mess for myself that might not have been fixable. Despite my parents, the shamans, the Equis, my future, and everything that all of that meant to me, I followed Cleo's gentle tug like a doll on a string.

Alana shoved a pair of my shoes against my chest. All four friends pulled me through the open panel in the glass wall and into the living area.

I pivoted to Cleo. "I didn't know you would—"

"Quiet," she whispered. "You don't want your parents waking."

Alana came close, and her soft, deep voice and breath entered my ear. "Especially since they'll ask questions about where we're going. Erikal wants it secret."

"Where *are* you—"

"Shhhh," Cleo and Alana said in unison.

The pair wrapped their arms beneath mine and moved me at a quick pace through the house. Erikal and Meritus followed. The main door slid up with a hiss.

"That door's so loud," Cleo whispered.

One crescent moon sat in the sky. Its dim, grey color suggested it was Palis, the darkest of all moons.

We couldn't possibly travel through unknown forests in such lightless conditions. "Thought you said it'd be brighter."

"It will be," Erikal said from behind. "Emba is rising now, and Hola will soon, then Dorel. All three full. It's only an hour to midnight."

That late already? If I had any shaman training, I could have read the sky and understood the time of night, but I had none. My father had never seen the magic in me.

The girls pulled me to Erikal's vehicle, lit by my home's small entry lamp. Seeing it up close made me believe I might have been dreaming. Its articulated exoskeleton followed natural curves and ridges like some mythical insect. But I hardly had a moment to take in Erikal's newest invention before he lifted me through its door—I was not small; he just had that strength.

"Isn't it amazing?" Meritus whispered to me from outside.

Without answering, I pushed my tired body onto a pile of

pillows on the floor.

Am I really going? Exhilaration and fear surged in me.

Several tiny green lamps blinked on throughout the oblong vaulted interior. The beauty of the complex chromadium-and-copper paneling struck me.

The vehicle consisted of little more than an empty carpeted floor and a control panel up front, like all cabs. But Cleo and Erikal had not exaggerated its size. Being spacious enough for us with plenty of room to spare, it had to be the largest in the Deo, and the first where the drivers could stand at the controls.

Meritus tossed me a piece of dried meat as he entered. "I helped him build it."

Cleo entered behind him. "We all helped." She took a sampling of his snack.

"I . . . really only helped prepare food," Alana said, grabbing the handholds and pulling herself onto the door's threshold.

"And you were excellent at that," Meritus said, sliding across the carpet to sit against the sidewall opposite me.

Alana dropped and leaned against him. "I made a lot. But only because I waited so long." She lifted her satchel.

Cleo looked at me. "It's been a running joke that I delayed everyone. It wasn't actually my fault. I couldn't sneak out. My parents were arguing forever in the main room."

Meritus snorted. "Those two statues? They have perfect stature. Perfect dress. Perfect things to say. Perfectly unable to fight."

"They argue," I said in Cleo's defense. "Renowned Mr. ArcGola can curse like a North Neighborhooder. I think he'd forget I was in the house sometimes."

"See?" Cleo said and mouthed a string of curses through a smile.

Everyone laughed.

"Yeah. Didn't foster a salubrious environment," I added.

Meritus shot me a look. "Didn't understand one word of that."

My cheeks turned hot. I sometimes forgot not to mimic the language of my favorite lore—*The Talik Stories*—which didn't require as much interpretation as most, if you understood the advanced grammar and vocabulary. Everyone laughed at Meritus's quip except Erikal, who tossed a waterskin to his friend. It hit hard against Meritus's chest, causing him to emit a grunt.

"It means the cursing wasn't nice to be around," Erikal said for me.

The joking around didn't make me forget, however, what I believed were Erikal's real reasons behind this trip—to be with the girl who'd mouthed the curses.

Cleo moved to the large forward windows, glancing over at me with an almost-embarrassed smile. *Was it because we talked about kissing?* She was genuinely pleased I was there, unlike Erikal, who didn't even look at me.

Alana gazed around the interior as though she hadn't yet seen it. She must have walked to my home. The design was shocking in its originality, but simple acknowledgment filled the girl's eyes more than wonder.

Meritus had introduced us to Alana only recently, just weeks before I started studying for the Equis, so I hadn't spent much time with her. She had seemed like a disquieted mystery, afraid to speak except when necessary. But she had talked much more when around only us, as though she'd gained the comfort of a yearslong friendship.

Erikal joined Cleo at the front. Their hands took the controls, her arms slender, his muscular, their bodies straight, confident, relaxed. It was as though they'd already driven together . . . a lot.

They adjusted the two wings' many facets to catch the invisible divine magic that rises from the ground. The imperceptible energy pushed on the facets, lifting the enormous cab. We rose several feet above the dew-soaked garden of my family's home. The vehicle levitated unusually high, maybe eight feet instead of the typical two or three.

Alana slid on her pillow as we rose. "Oh, the Sun!"

The sudden movement sent a jolt up my spine. "How high does it go?"

Erikal stuck his hand out as if gauging our elevation. "This is about it." The machine's exterior Sunfire lights remained deactivated. Even so, Meritus and Alana watched through the side windows as we silently floated away from the earthen berm of my home.

We were off, following the Deo Stream and travelling only by the light of occasional home-entry lamps.

In the faint green interior lighting, my friends' clothes stood out. Curving, colorful, amorphous shapes like twisting teardrops, meandering lines, and eggs covered their entire outfits. Bizarre. They must have been Cleo's designs. Apparently, she had been making more extravagant textile patterns. Only I wore our traditional Deoan clothes with a few rigid blue lines around the shoulders, arms, and waist.

I had been away from them for four months and, suddenly, they'd made recorders, giant cabs, and eccentric clothes.

"You look confused," Meritus said. "I suppose you didn't think we'd come get you?"

"Had a feeling," I lied.

"Of course he did," Alana said. Her thick, wavy hair covered much of her face, as it often had, her eyes tucked halfway behind the thicket. "Giels has shaman blood in him."

"Ooh," Meritus said, "predicting the future, are you?"

I smiled. "Hardly." I didn't know if Alana really believed I could predict the future, but I knew Meritus teased me. "I found out you needed my recorder for wherever you're going," I said, to see if I could expose that the trip wasn't actually about the message they put in it. "Risky plan leaving it with me."

Meritus shrugged and tossed a piece of dried meat in his mouth. "If you refused to join us, we'd have sweet-talked it from you."

"We're glad you came," Erikal said, turning from the controls. "Your knowledge of lore might be handy."

"'Lore?'" I said, but no one responded. Did Erikal genuinely want me there? What lore would he expect to give insight on the message? Was he really going to try and make me believe it was mystical? The thing was, with my knowledge of lore, I could have probably exposed holes in any mystical reasons he may have for this trip.

My body straightened. I understood why Tohillocen had focused my attention on the device. She'd found a way out of this adventure without Cleo thinking less of me. My first instinct had been right. The message, the entire reason for going, clearly wasn't mystical, and I could prove it.

I searched my mind for a relevant phrase from ancient history. One from the uncommonly recited lore *Karranae's Dissolution* bubbled up in my mind.

In mortal flesh, you now be. Separated from spirit, thee. The heavens and Underworld cannot speak to you in word.

In the passage, the immortals described one of many changes lesser souls could expect when they first became living mortals. The last phrase echoed inside me—"Cannot speak to you in word."

Ever since mortals had ascended from the Underworld to the world between the earth and sky, the spiritual realm and gods could guide and even influence people, especially shamans, but they did so wordlessly, inspiring feelings and thoughts during meditation, as well as with weather.

Immortal beings did not communicate directly with living mortals by speaking, including with messages on a recorder. Storytellers generally understood this. My father had even once confirmed to me the notion was an official shaman's judgment, even though many people still believed spirits and gods talked to them in dreams.

I rolled my eyes. How had I not thought of it sooner?

Slowly at first, then all at once, heat surged in my face. If Cleo wouldn't be furious for my sake, I had good reason to be. With the phony message, either Meritus or Erikal, or both, were toying with my life.

But instead of saying something, I pushed my tongue into my cheek and threw my arms behind my head. Being able to show the message was a hoax, thus having an out whenever it suited me, I decided to enjoy a short ride. Why not? I'd just make it seem like the logic occurred to me as we chatted about it, a conversation I'd start up in just a moment.

Everything would work out—with me doing my rehearsal, with Cleo seeing my adventurousness. Relief washed over me like the Deo Stream's cool water.

However, I still didn't know our destination. Besides just my curiosity, it could have exposed more flaws in Erikal's reasoning.

"Does anyone plan to tell me where you're going? The Lost Forest?"

Cleo turned. A slight smile pushed up her smooth cheeks. She held me with her bright gaze as if to build up my anticipation. "*We're* going to the cave," she said, as sweet as syrup. Based on her casual tone, she might as well have been saying "to a friend's house." But I knew what she referred to—the Wind Cave. One of the most sacred places in the World, if not *the* most sacred.

That was farther than the Lost Forest.

Chills ran down my arms.

Our traditional stories often talked about the Wind Cave's magic and dangers, and the impossibility of entering. Only shamans, on rare occasions, took the long trek to visit its entrance for prayer and ceremony. No other Deoans had gone to look at the sacred opening—not recently, anyway. My father wouldn't elaborate, but he'd said the shamans hadn't travelled that way in a generation because the trek had become extremely dangerous.

Erikal's explanation for going *there* would be interesting.

Cleo had called Elder Sparus a loon, but Erikal was starting to make him look sane. I'd be doing my friends a huge favor by ending this trip.

We now drove in complete darkness. No more entry lights dotted the view, suggesting we'd left the Deo. It seemed fast. Too fast. Homes sat along the stream to about eight miles out, and going beyond them should have taken many times as long.

I pressed my face against the glass to verify. It would have been the furthest west I'd ever been.

Although no more lights popped into view, the darkness didn't last. As Erikal had predicted, the moonlight indeed brightened.

Through the break in the forest canopy over the stream, I occasionally caught glimpses of four moons, including the two brightest, Emba and Hola. The forest transformed into shades of grey. Nighttimes that light were rare.

The scene held my attention. The unfamiliar forest's moonlit foliage, glistening with dew, rushed by in a continuous hypnotic rhythm.

* * *

A thunderous clap awakened me. I touched everything nearby, completely disoriented, thinking I should've been in my room.

No dreams had come to me, I'd slept so deep—as though I'd fallen unconscious.

Erikal's cab bobbed up and down, and it had grown light outside. Grey clouds pockmarked the blue sky. Somewhere beyond sight, a thunderstorm raged.

"Where are we?" I asked. "What time is it?" I sat up, my eyes darting around and my heart pounding. How many hours had I lost?

We travelled over a large stream in a deep gorge, its sides laden with moss and flora. Trees towered in the forest above.

"Good morning," Cleo said. "Deo Stream, still, but six or so hours downstream. Much further than we've ever been. We're not going west anymore. Did you know the stream turned northwards?" I shook my head, even though I'd heard that.

We'd only travelled a few hours. The absolute latest I could have them turn around would be late afternoon. I didn't want to wait, but I allowed for a quick moment to take in the astounding sheer rock faces on either side. The Deo was almost entirely flat, nothing like the impossible verticality of the land here. How did it not fall on us?

Meritus and Alana stretched and rubbed their eyes as though they had just awakened also.

"Wow," Meritus said. "What people say is true—the stream does get bigger."

The roaring waterway splashed and dropped with white water, but the cab only bobbed slightly above it all.

Down the gorge's sides, water fell like hairy tails or poured like showers.

"Waterfalls!" I shouted and pointed, completely taken in by the scene. I had never before seen one.

"You've already missed some big ones," Cleo said.

Now that I was fully awake, the realization clicked how far my friends said we'd travel. The cave was much farther than a couple of days. I let out a scoff. "You're joking about the cave. The Equis is in two weeks, and you know I need to get back, right?"

"That's why we're hurrying," Erikal said. Focused on driving, he didn't turn to look at me.

Because Erikal had planned the trip with Cleo during my rehearsal tomorrow, exposing his ruse would be deserved. Not exposing him would be too generous, but maybe I wouldn't need to embarrass him to return. "I can't go. It's a week just to get there. You know I can't be gone that long."

"I think Erikal's trying to prove something, like it's a challenge," Meritus said. "Why else try to get back in three days?"

"What is a foregone conclusion cannot be a challenge," Erikal said.

"Three days? There *and* back? That's impossible." I looked to Meritus for agreement.

He shrugged one shoulder.

Despite Erikal's talent for designing on the computer, no cab had come close to the speed he suggested. A paranoia creeped in that he *did* have ulterior motives—that he wanted to sabotage me by keeping me from my studies for weeks. *But why would he do that? He's one of my best friends and says he wants me here.* Then again, if he had designs on Cleo, perhaps he'd gained an advantage whether I came or not.

The sky shifted to grey, and whirling plumes of dark, angry clouds accosted the mountain peaks above the gorge. Tohillocen, the shadow goddess of rain, poured with a fury.

Thunder from Etargoren, the great generator and god of power, rolled across the land and vibrated the vehicle's floor.

"The esteemed elders are deciding your fate, huh?" Meritus said, and tossed me a slice of cured meat. I hit it with my palm, and it ricocheted back. He tried to catch it with his mouth but missed.

"If it's all fate, I wouldn't worry about getting back," I said.

Meritus turned to the drivers. "See, Erikal? Told you he wouldn't go if you gave away where we're going."

Cleo spun around, her eyes wide with genuine surprise. "*You knew?*"

Meritus threw his arms behind his head. "Figured it out days ago."

I scoffed. "You're right. I wouldn't go that far, putting myself in danger, based on a prank message." I had meant to be more tactful, but it just came out.

"Oh! It's not a prank after all," Cleo said. "Ask Erikal."

"It's not a prank," Erikal said.

I rolled my eyes. "Like you said, I know lore. It's not hard to prove—"

A nearby thunderclap jolted me. Every one of us cried out,

followed by Cleo and Erikal laughing.

A knot formed in my stomach. It wasn't funny.

Rainwater cascaded down the cab's windows, blurring our view, which only happened in the heaviest of downpours thanks to the water-shedding properties of windscreen glass. Raging stream water dribbled through the vehicle's side vents, wetting the floor. Erikal activated the bright exterior Sunfire lamps, but the added light did little. From the blurred view, it looked like the stream funneled through perfectly vertical cliffs.

"Water's coming in," I said. "Why are you so low?"

"Can't fly any higher," Cleo said. "It's the ground we levitate above, not the water. The stream's so deep." Water now pounded through the vents as waves hit us, wetting the carpet and my behind.

"This ride has been fun," I said, not intending to sound as sarcastic as I did, "but find a place to stop."

Erikal pressed his face close to a windshield pane. "Nowhere to do that."

"Then turn around."

"Can't. The waves are battering us from the rear. We might get a little soaked."

My stomach churned as they continued pushing through the narrow gorge. I should have been focused on the danger, but I couldn't let the subject of our destination drop. "Why in the world between the earth and sky would you go to the cave?"

"It could be a human spirit in the recorder," Alana said, just loud enough to hear above the storm.

A human spirit? A ghost? Is that what Erikal told them? This was getting more absurd.

The torrent swelled the Deo Stream and its tributaries. The cab continued to bob up and down, struggling to hover above the rapids. Water poured in, inundating the carpet. I stood.

It was time to end this.

"Friends, lore is very clear that spirits, human or otherwise, do not talk to mortals with words. The message can't be real."

"*The Journey to Salihandron*," Alana said, staring at me.

Salihandron? *Hell.*

"It's one of my favorite stories. Don't you know it?" Alana said.

"Yes, of course." Heat rose to my face from embarrassment, followed by a quick shot of fear up my spine. Focusing so much on embarrassing Erikal, I'd forgotten about that terrifying god's quirk. The Death Escort, the Messenger, the Great Breath. Deities merely influenced the mortal World from afar, *except* Salihandron. He, she, or it had no corporeal form, only illusions, and was the one immortal being who could speak to mortals in our languages.

The Journey to Salihandron was a frightening story few wished to know. I did, of course. Apparently, Alana knew it, too. And, uncomfortably, her interpretation of the recorder's message seemed to fit. I quoted from a story to remind my friends and myself of the lore:

> *Salihandron's first message came to Takka. The warrior saw a shadow where no person stood. The shadow spoke, "You have risen from below and found the mortal World. For the World to have peace over time, all mortal souls must eventually return home and forget. I, Salihandron, alone shall summon every spirit back. Mortal-kind cannot avoid my words. The receivers must abide, and their spirits return."*

"That's exactly why I'm glad you're here," Erikal said, "your word-for-word, detailed knowledge of history, which seems to confirm what Alana suspected."

Meritus put his palm to his mouth. "Yawn. Sounds like a bunch of words thrown together."

A thunderclap vibrated the cab. "You're supposed to *think* about the meaning," I said. "It helps to know a number of stories."

Cleo turned with a gleam in her eye. "So, enlighten us."

I paused to think, hoping to come up with a way to disprove that Salihandron had talked to us. I rubbed my forehead. Nothing came to mind, so I explained the traditional interpretation of the passage. "It means death and rebirth maintain the World's balance. But, also, if the message is Salihandron's, it would be wise for us to follow what it says. In fact, we have no choice."

"Whoa," Meritus said. "So we *have* to go to the cave?"

I shook my head. "Of course not. *Only* if the message is real and from Salihandron. Even then, you'd have to interpret the words correctly."

Water continued sloshing through the vents, so much so that several inches covered the floor. Pillows floated about like leaves on a calm stream. All of us stood now, except for Alana, who shimmied around to close the vents. But water still seeped in, if more slowly. She finally stood, soaked. I averted my eyes as her clothes clung to her skin.

Quickly, the interior became suffocatingly stuffy. Lightning flashed over and over beyond the rain's veil. Booms echoed.

I fought my growing nausea.

"Cleo, Erikal," Alana said, "can you *please* find a place to stop?" She held her hand to her mouth as though she also resisted queasiness.

The vehicle's swaying ceased. I was about to thank them before noticing that we were still moving forwards.

"No need to worry," Cleo said, wiping her forehead with a trembling hand. "The water's flattened out." Through the blurred front view, a dark, flat surface winded within the brown and green of the gorge. The rain still poured, but at least we hovered through it calmly.

"Alana came up with the idea," Meritus shouted at me over the rain. He popped another piece of meat in his mouth. "It's why we're out here."

"What idea?"

"That there's a human spirit in the recorder," he said through his chewing. "Erikal's going along with it. Alana's really fond of ghosts, I think. I'm just excited to see the world."

My entire body shivered, either from Meritus's words, the cold, or both. Alana thought the recorder had captured a human spirit, a mortal soul—a ghost? Nothing in lore would refute that idea on its own, especially if Salihandron had left the message. It explained going to the Wind Cave, since lost souls exit the mortal World there at Salihandron's behest.

I had never heard of a device containing a human spirit, though. Then again, no one had owned a recorder before.

My friends were more adept at lore than I recalled. Did they actually believe Salihandron sought our help transporting a lost soul? Could the message have not been a prank? "So, do you plan to toss the recorder into the cave or something?"

"It's an option," Erikal said.

"That's what I suggested," Alana said. "I came because I wanted to witness it."

The rain fell in ever-thickening sheets.

Glints of Alana's eyes peeked out through locks of her wavy

hair. I couldn't tell if she was looking at me. "What gives you the idea the recorder trapped a human soul?" I asked her.

"A recorder is a vessel for thought without form," she said. "Is that not what a body is to a soul? It seems a soul could exist in either."

I screwed my face up. I had to admit, she had an imagination. Though as insightful as her idea sounded, it was easily fanciful. And she just gave me a way to solve this supposed problem for them. Like dead bodies, machine spirits, and presumably human souls, couldn't live in dismantled machines. "Can't we just take the recorder apart? That should free the ghost, and it can find its own way to—wherever. No need to go to the cave."

"We can't. As part of its creation, I had to make it indestruc-tible." Erikal said it so casually, as though making devices indestructible was normal.

Cleo and I looked at each other knowingly. Was that why the delicate petals had not been damaged when she'd dropped it? But the idea of an indestructible machine was too absurd. "Now you're definitely putting me on."

"Nope. That's how the computer-spirit wanted it," Erikal said. "The diagrams didn't give me any other option. Anyhow, it's not clear what to do. I can interpret the message in ten ways."

Rubbing my forehead, I turned from my friends. The outside world had become nothing but water and grey: rain, falls, and river. A blurred bolt of lightning flashed nearby. The cracking of thick wood echoed, followed by the scraping of a broken tree falling to its doom in a crash nearby. I pushed my hand through my hair.

Perhaps with the calm water, we could now stop. "Tohillocen doesn't seem to want us to go forwards," I said, even though I had no idea of the god's intent.

Meritus hung from two ceiling handholds, with his knees bent to keep his feet above the sloshing water below. He swayed from the cab's movement like a tree creature. "Well, the gods must be having an argument. Salihandron beckons us forwards, and Tohillocen wants us to return. What did you say, Giels? With Salihandron, we have no choice? It seems we go onwards."

"Onwards!" Cleo echoed.

I could have just shouted at them to turn around, but I wanted Cleo to believe I had the interest and boldness for this trip. Anyhow, I still had time, and none of this made sense. I took a deep breath. "If a mortal's spirit is in my recorder, how did it get there?"

"My best guess," Erikal said, "is that, when creating the object, the computer-spirit pulled an entity from the ether. That's the normal process of giving machines life and bringing the machine-spirit into them. But Alana's right. It's plausible that instead of a machine-spirit, a mortal soul might be captured by something as magical as a recorder. Maybe Salihandron saw an opportunity to place a wayward ghost in there." That was the first time he'd called the recorder a magic item, which confirmed my assumption that it was unique and powerful.

I raised my palms. "You made it. How can you not know how it works?"

"The computer-spirit's fickle. We don't get to see *all* its secrets. Maybe the Talis will know what to do."

He would bring the Talis into this? Their reputation for spiritual depth and knowledge of magic preceded them. "The Talis? Are they there?"

"They're coastal people, and the cave is on the coast," Erikal said.

The cab lifted, and the water poured away through the vents, leaving behind a soaked mess of carpet and pillows. Tired from keeping my balance, I kneeled with my back against the sidewall. Another fear rose in me: Erikal had never gone to the cave before. "How do you know if we're going the right way? I doubt a normal cab would've made it back there."

"I talked to several knowledgeable people," Erikal said, "including the Treespeaker and Elder Treehaven. I asked them to describe distant lands as they saw fit—you know, so they wouldn't be suspicious. From that, I pieced together a map in my mind. But we're not going the usual way during this leg, which is near the Lost Forest—didn't like the sound of that place, with the Lost Tribe and all."

Now, I wished I hadn't asked. Erikal tended to go on, as if he were a tribal leader himself, educating the young.

"We shouldn't worry too much about the storm in this vehicle," he continued. "It has a stiff frame. This way will bring us to the Camchaw River, connecting back to the usual route, which leads directly to the coast. And, there, the Talis can tell us how we can give the soul to Salihandron."

We can give the soul? It occurred to me Salihandron having us deliver a soul to the god would be contrary to its essence.

My body relaxed. The beginnings of an idea formed as to why the god hadn't talked to us and why this trip was futile—and why we should turn back now. Time pressed on, so I opened my mouth to talk it through.

A strange look of horror on Alana's face stopped me.

She stood, her half-concealed eyes staring out the front, filled with fire.

"I hope this was the hardest part," Meritus said, not noticing Alana. "We're soaked."

Alana's arm rose in an undead fashion, like a stiff log, pointing ahead.

"Should have been," Erikal said, "except for maybe one spot. Ever hear of Ceridia?"

"Stop!" Alana yelled. "The earth is ending."

5

Stars in the Sky

The cab's sudden stop jolted me forwards over soaked pillows. I landed on my elbows and slid across the cab's wet carpet, burning my skin. "Ow."

Alana caught a handhold while still pointing through the front window.

Cleo turned to her. "Why'd we stop?"

"The earth ends!" Alana said. "Don't go forwards. We'll die."

I almost laughed, I thought the idea so ridiculous. And how could she see through all the condensation?

Cleo and Erikal immediately folded up the wings to stabilize the craft.

The storm roared magnitudes louder than moments before.

To clear the air, Alana opened the main door, which rotated on its top hinges. Rainwater poured off as it rose to become a canopy. The roar grew more deafening than any rain.

Meritus defogged the front windscreens with his shirtsleeves, clearing the view.

"Ceridia, the angry waterfall," Erikal said. He turned to Alana, looking unusually humbled with his head dropped a bit. "Alana, thanks. Amazing eyesight. I missed it. We need to get to the bank. Quick."

Through the cleared windows, the world did not end, but the river appeared to. I stared, uncertain of what to do. The waterfall's ledge came closer; we still moved forwards.

Meritus flicked switches while Cleo and Erikal handled other controls.

The cab turned, but we continued moving towards the drop-off. Alana and I stood motionless, paralyzed. Having little experience driving cabs, let alone this complicated one, I could offer no help.

Erikal glanced at the vents, where water sporadically poured in. "The waves are pushing us." He turned to the open door and pointed at the forested rock bank to the left of the falls. "Over there, the rock cliff."

Cleo glanced over. "What about the trees?"

"Don't worry about the trees. Meritus, take over my controls. I've an idea." Erikal jumped to the door.

"The do-it-all?" Cleo asked.

"No, can't get to it. Rotate both wings port side. Quickly. Grab the cliff."

"Okay! Meritus, you fan out the plates; I'll crank the trusses," Cleo said. "Everyone, hold on."

The cab jolted. Alana screamed. Before I knew it, her arms were around my waist, her wet clothes soaking mine. I wrapped my arm around her shoulder. "It'll be fine," I said, as much to comfort myself as Alana.

My nausea returned.

Cleo's stance widened, and her right arm furiously rotated a crank, her entire body leaning into it. "Come on." Her normal elegance evaporated into pure aggression.

Meritus worked at other controls, his hands flying all over the panel.

Rain blew in the opened door, soaking Erikal. Holding the jamb with one hand, he swung his other hand to reach far out, as if to grab the scrubby trees clinging to the rock bank, but several feet lay between them and his fingers. Slowly, a long, horizontal branch came into view while the waves pounded us towards the drop.

We're going to fall.

I opened my mouth to curse at Erikal about the foolishness of this trip. But it would've made things much worse. With Alana under my arm, thankfully I kept control.

Erikal grunted and extended his reach to the limb. "Sathunedri must have it in for us!" he said, invoking the goddess of falling water. I closed my eyes for a moment, praying to her.

Erikal grabbed the branch and held firm, but his other hand slipped on the door's smooth metal jamb. He pulled hard.

My paralysis passed, and I jumped to Erikal and grabbed his slipping arm. Alana braced against the interior wall and held his wrist.

Partly visible from my vantage, both wing assemblies, now on the left side over the door, smashed against wet branches above. The cab shook. My hands slipped on Erikal's soaked arm. I grabbed his sleeve and heard it rip.

The rock cliff rose on our left. With a deep yell and holding tight to the branch, Erikal yanked us towards it. The waves, angry and virulent, pushed us to the waterfall's edge. Each of the wings' many facets rotated on their pivots until the two wing assemblies resembled talons. Those claws found a rock ledge—narrow, but the earth's levitating power coming through was just enough to keep the entire cab in the air.

"Oh, the Sun! Hold on, Erikal!" Alana screamed.

"Cleo, Meritus," Erikal said, his voice a growl. "You've got it. Hang us off the side without bumping the trees."

I looked down, but shouldn't have. Roaring water dropped like falling stones to a dark, swirling pool a hundred feet below. I stumbled back. Erikal's arm had moved. Before I fell to the floor, a hand caught my sleeve—Erikal's.

"We're fine now," he said, and let me go.

"What?" I couldn't help myself. I stepped to the open door and glanced down again. Nothing lay between us and the dark water and rocks below. My head grew light.

Erikal pulled the door shut. Through the windows, the outer facets of both wing assemblies extended to the left and floated just above the small, crooked rock ledge while we, in the cab's hull, stuck well out into the air. The entire vehicle cantilevered off the ends of the wings. The meandering ledge, in places only a foot wide, slowly descended to the lower river, just beyond Ceridia's whirling pool. Erikal joined the other drivers and, with only the wingtips harnessing the floating power of the earth, we descended alongside the ledge to safety.

Cheers erupted from all of us. I could not have been more stunned. "We did it," I said in absolute amazement. I turned to look back at the falls in hopes of seeing the most impressive sight of my life, but Erikal hadn't included windows in the back of the vehicle. We could only see where we were going, not where we'd been.

"We would certainly have plummeted to our deaths," Erikal said, "in a whirlpool of cold. Thank you again, Alana."

"Erikal, thank *you*." Alana sounded breathless.

Erikal had been wearing my nerves, but he'd just reminded me why I admired him so much. In the moment, I let it slide that we would not have been in danger if not for him.

Cleo turned to me, and we hugged. "You're fantastic," I told her. "How'd you learn to drive like that?"

She smiled, her eyes filling with glowing pride. But dark rings surrounded them.

"I think you've earned a rest," I said.

"Oh, I'm much too energized now."

Meritus leaned with his back against the control panel. "Sathunedri wanted us to fall down Ceridia, but we got the better of her."

"Tohillocen and Etargoren have wanted us to stop, too," Cleo said. "Yet we've gotten through it without getting hurt at all. Maybe Salihandron helped."

Alana looked at me. "Is it possible? Salihandron is guiding us as we thought?"

I understood the rush of emotions, but my friends were jumping to conclusions. For all we knew, Tohillocen created the storm to somehow punish or help a nearby tribe. "I don't know. It's tough understanding whether their actions are meant for us."

"All things are connected," Cleo said.

"I know, but that doesn't necessarily mean it's true just because we think a certain way about it. Shamans are the ones who can best interpret such things." I might have been killing the mood, but I didn't care.

Meritus casually chewed at a fingernail and eyed me. "So, you don't think gods are battling us and Salihandron for the recorder-ghost's fate?"

"Personally, I wouldn't assume—" I started, but decided to let it go.

More worldly concerns nagged at me. We had nearly died.

By the looks of the river ahead, we were no longer in jeopardy. I took in a deep breath to gather myself. "Will we be able to return back up the falls?"

Erikal, now driving, turned his head a fraction towards me. "Not in this weather."

Even in the heavy rain, I could tell the day edged towards mid-afternoon. We would have needed to turn around soon to make it back in time, but with the raging storm and waterfall, that seemed unlikely.

My shock from nearly falling did not abate. It only transformed to realizing I might not return today. What would my parents say? Would the council shun me? For the first time, I wished I believed in the adventure—to distract from my idiocy in joining them.

Fatigue enveloped me. I slid down the wall to the wet floor, resigned to being thankful that Ceridia had not killed Cleo and me, and our friends.

Cleo came and sat at my side, her head resting on my shoulder. And, after an exhausted exhale, she fell asleep.

My heart thumped.

Did we really need to come out here, Cleo? Was it worth ruining my future?

How could everything change so easily?

I wrapped an arm around Cleo to keep her warm. Her eyes softened to delicate horizontal lines crowned by long, brown lashes. My future wife. I still thought it a safe assumption; after all, she had promised a kiss. Maybe the journey wouldn't be a complete setback.

Alana looked at me curiously and smiled. Perhaps she saw my passing contentment.

Our pace quickened over the river's gravelly shore. Instead

of moving at the speed of a slow jog like other cabs, we darted faster than the quickest Deoan sprinter. The power of Erikal's vehicle astounded me.

For a while, I gazed absently at the trees, rain, and mist.

* * *

The Deo Stream grew into a small river and merged with a much larger waterway.

"This must be the Camchaw River," Erikal said to Meritus. The river, at least forty feet wide, was of a size none of us had ever seen. With the sight, the reality of our adventure returned.

Though I didn't believe the gods fought over us, I did wonder what *was* going on.

Erikal had made a recorder, a mythical item only mentioned in the most rarefied informal legends. Despite the fascinating promise such a device would hold, no one had ever created one—at least to my knowledge—suggesting it took extraordinary skill.

And there was the message. Alana believed Salihandron had placed a ghost within the device, and that the god had created the message to prompt us to bring it to the Wind Cave.

She'd invented quite a narrative for such a vague message. Maybe the council's concerns over Erikal's inventions stemmed from Alana's theory, if they had heard it. Meritus might have told Elder Sparus to stir him up.

I wanted to ask Erikal if he knew that the shamans had been talking about him. Was that why he had kept our destination a secret and why we had sneaked off at night? But I wouldn't ask, both because my father had told me not to discuss the council's concerns and because Erikal had a habit of divining any hidden intent behind questions. They held me in a vise of secrets—him on one side, the council on the other.

Pulling the recorder out of my pocket, I pressed the back button. Erikal seemed to instinctively glance at me, watching as I struggled with the device. It wouldn't go back to the strange message. He stepped over, took the recorder, and pressed the button repeatedly, as if with an asynchronous rhythm. Suddenly, the machine recited the message to me for a second time:

"Can you hear me? This is what we've been waiting for. From the ether, you have found me. We are of the other world. Return me through the passage."

He deactivated the device.

"It sounds like the recorder is talking to us about itself," I said, looking straight at Alana. "But you think it's Salihandron asking us to escort a ghost in the machine?"

"If Erikal didn't put it there, who else and for what other reason?"

Erikal looked at me, holding a stern expression. At that moment, I stopped believing he or Meritus had intentionally created the message. Erikal's disposition was too straightforward to maintain such a lie after we'd been in mortal danger. I stared out the window for a while, watching the skinny, unfamiliar trees on the bank, allowing myself to accept that the message wasn't a ruse. But an immortal? I shook my head.

If it were an immortal who'd created the message, Alana had made an intelligent guess as to who. No other being in the pantheon could send a direct, audible message across worlds. At least, not that I was aware.

But before we had arrived at the waterfall, I realized her idea had a major flaw. Salihandron had never sent mortals to do errands, as escorting souls to the other realm was the essence of the god's existence. To be philosophical about it, as I understood it from my father's explanation of the lore, the very act of transporting ghosts made the god come into being and, concurrently, the god coming into being made the act.

"What do we do with the recorder if the Talis aren't there to help us figure this out?" I asked, noticing the weary frustration in my own voice. "Has anyone thought of that?"

Erikal tossed the device back to me. "I have a thousand ideas. But no sense in boring you."

"Any favorites?"

"My idea," Meritus said, "is that Salihandron will turn into a giant shadow by the cave and eat us alive."

Alana reached out and smacked his side. "Not funny."

Meritus laughed. "Could happen. And, aside from the eating us alive part, it'd be amazing."

"If the Talis aren't there, giving the recorder to the cave might be a top choice," Erikal said. "Assuming this is Salihandron's work, the answer should come to us."

I let out a long, exaggerated, sigh. I didn't understand how two people as intelligent as Erikal and Cleo could get whipped up in a specious, mystical frenzy. In all likelihood, the message was a result of a computer glitch, which happened sometimes. In retrospect, that could have been what Tohillocen had wanted me to understand all along when I had prayed to her in the courtyard.

Red clay cliffs, half-covered in scrub and grasses, banked the river on both sides. Above the cliffs, trees rose like ghosts into the dimming, grey sky. Far ahead, stars blinked into existence within a patchwork of indigo. The clouds ahead had started to thin, though rain continued to hit the glass.

In the growing darkness, the Sunfire lights illuminated the entire area nearby.

Movement near the shore caught my eye. "See any people?" I asked the drivers.

Meritus took his hands off the controls and leaned forwards. "No, but what have we here?"

Tazers, a sort of flying lizard, swirled in massive numbers above the Camchaw River. They engulfed us. I had only seen them once before, during the short journey my father and I had taken when I was a child. At the time, he had cautioned me about them.

Many of the arm-length beasts landed and crawled on the windows, squawking and completely covering the view. Erikal and Meritus swatted at the glass to scare them off, to no effect.

Meritus pulled a spear out of a compartment. "If anyone can ground one of these, it's you." He tossed me the aluminum weapon.

"You give me too much credit," I said, trying to sound humble.

He grabbed the door handle. "C'mon, try."

"They're terrible game," I said. "They're peaceful until you're a threat." To my relief, Meritus moved away from the door, and Erikal stopped hitting the windscreen.

Perhaps because they garnered no further attention from the cab's inhabitants, the tempest of flying lizards darted away.

"See, Giels?" Meritus said. "Every time danger comes our way, we easily escape it. If this is not the work of Salihandron, how do you explain it?"

"If I'd not been here, you'd wish you'd fallen into the pool of Ceridia instead of having those beasts tear into you."

"But you are here," Alana said.

I rubbed my temple. My friends' fantasies caused my head to

sear. "Alana, Erikal, Meritus, you're creating this in your minds. Salihandron does not make mortals into couriers."

Meritus screwed up his face. "But you're not a shaman, so how could *you* know?"

I did not know why, exactly, but the childish comment stung.

"Fine, you're correct, I'm not a shaman, which is to my point that the only thing we can do about the message is to let the council interpret it. Erikal, it's ridiculous to think any of us know what to do. At best, it's an error of your making. At worst, a horrid omen."

Erikal turned to me. He did not look offended, but quizzical. "I don't make mistakes on the computer, Giels." He winked.

I laughed despite myself. *Why did I laugh?*

He'd made me feel too severe, even though he'd said he wanted me here for lore. Unbelievable.

A lock of hair ran across Cleo's sleeping face. I moved it aside.

Searching for something positive to look forward to on our trip, I held out hope the cave would be worthwhile. But I estimated we'd need to trudge another day or two, cold and soaked, before finding out.

More stars came into view, and the rain slowed to a drizzle.

I craned my neck. A cloudless sky formed in the distance, meaning the bad weather would soon pass. My heart lifted. Perhaps we could, in fact, return in time if we rushed. But I'd need to convince them to go back now, which might not be easy.

"Oh, the Sun," I said to myself.

Alana looked at me, her brow furrowed tight.

Would it be worth ending this, waking Cleo and demanding we return? Could any of us know how difficult Ceridia would be to scale and how long that would take? And was there a chance Erikal and Alana sensed something about the meaning of the message? I doubted it. But as Meritus insinuated, unlike shamans, I'd never received training on interpreting lore beyond the council's official judgments. I only recited the stories.

Uncertainty weighed on me, but I needed to do something. "Erikal."

He turned again, this time with a sparkle in his eyes. I hesitated. His look of delight and overall confidence made me want to believe in everything my friends did.

I pushed that away. "If Tohillocen calms the weather, how long would it take to return now, going upstream and up Ceridia?"

He gave me a broad smile. "Return now, my friend? When we're here?"

Here? Impossible.

Some distance downstream, the valley gave way to an endless, roiling plane of water. My eyes followed it farther and farther until they stopped on the true end of the world, where the sea met the twilight of the darkening sky.

"The Western Sea," Erikal said, probably in response to my awe.

He nudged Meritus and pointed up the steep embankment on the south side, which rose at least two tall trees' height.

The driving pair pushed the cab up an old trail of switchbacks on the incline.

I whispered in Cleo's ear for her to awaken. Her eyes blinked open and she sat up, taking in the view. She exhaled a breath of surprise.

Cresting over the top, we arrived on the fabled Boromount Plateau, named for the giant beasts that lived there. But despite its name, I knew of the place more for the cave.

A grassy plain strewn with dark boulders sloped gently away from us. In the far distance, black creatures hulked on four legs. I scanned for the cave, expecting to see an immense hole in the earth, perhaps with a torrent of magic mist and dust flying about it, or something just as impressive.

Erikal pointed to a towering rock outcropping of spires at the mesa's western edge. "There."

We approached, floating over the tall grasses. The rock spires straddled the edge of the plateau where it dropped in a cliff to the Western Sea. At the bottom of the outcropping, where it met the plateau, sat a modest black opening.

Erikal slapped an empty part of the control panel several times with excitement. "Call her the Silver Dare! She's brought us out here." Indeed, no other cab could have taken us here so quickly.

The drivers stopped us about a hundred feet from the spires. Alana lifted the door. Anxious to be done with this, I led us out. We fell silent in the cool, dark air.

Few grasses grew near the cave, and those that did fluttered with anger. Wind howled from the black aperture, whipping at my hair, even at our distance. Power infused the noise and colored the entire scene.

The moon gods Emba, Hola, and Dorel had not yet risen, but their pale light glowed over the ridgeline to the east and played upon the waves on the sea and dew-soaked grasses around our feet. Our homeland, and most of the world between the earth and sky, was dense forest. Above us, we saw for the first time a sky unimpeded by trees, glistening with endless stars—the lesser gods and souls of soon-to-be newborn mortals. They rested in the velvet robes of Morgoreth, the great veil of the night.

The place overwhelmed me with feelings of unreality, like I

was looking through someone else's eyes. But I did not. We were there. We made it to the most mystical and awesome place, and in hardly any time.

The Silver Dare's wings, made up of curving metal panels of varying sizes like a string of leaves, connected by struts shaped like thin bones, picked up pale glints from the moonglow like the waves and grasses.

And my friends' faces, like the wings, seemed to cull the light of the heavens. It was not only their faces that I saw shine at that moment, but their very selves. The grandeur of the night accentuated my awareness of them. I watched their wonder and curiosity, and, feeling so overcome, comparisons between them and the bright stars—the lesser gods—came to mind unbidden.

I did not compare my friends to minor gods casually. Something I'd always believed resurfaced, breaking through my sourness of earlier: they would change the Deo. And I sensed this adventure could be the start of it.

"Makes it seem like we're special," Meritus said, as if seeing into my mind, "being here—like we can do anything together . . . go anywhere."

We all nodded. Erikal even cracked a smile. We must have all felt the same thing, and with my surge of inspiration, I pushed all regret aside.

Seeing no signs of the Talis tribe, perhaps I should have given my unique gift to Salihandron as my friends had suggested, so we could be done with this adventure. But after just a single step forward towards the distant cave, I stopped. The raw energy of the cave's windy howl sent chills all over me. I gestured for Erikal to take the machine.

"The wind might be too strong to throw it in," he said, with an apparent change of heart. "Keep it. I have a new idea."

I didn't deserve the item. Meritus had been correct. Without shamanistic training, such an unusual thing would be beyond my understanding. Again, I held it out for Eirkal to take it, but while looking at the night sky, he raised his palm. I didn't question him further. I found it odd he refused, considering all of his effort in coming out here. But it meant I would have the device longer, and I liked it despite the strange voice.

Erikal's gaze fell onto the Silver Dare. "I wonder if Meritus is right that we can go anywhere. Let's go."

I sucked in the strange sea air to have a last taste as we filed back into the cab. I'd done it. I'd shown Cleo I could be as adventurous as any of them—as adventurous as Erikal. And perhaps we could return in time for my rehearsal, but we had no room for delays. Closing my eyes for a moment, I gave a prayer to Glosa, the goddess of hope, balance, and the air.

Sitting inside the vehicle, I waited for Erikal to turn us back home or explain why we hadn't rid ourselves of my machine.

But he did neither. "Let's see if she can do it," he said under his breath, and shoved a lever forwards, pushing the vehicle at its fastest speed towards the cave.

"Erikal?" I said, and shot up.

A gust hit us hard, jolting the cab. But Erikal didn't stop.

The rock spires and the black entrance at their base drew closer. My eyes must have grown as round as moons. The others reacted the same. "Erikal!" I shouted. "What're you doing?"

Alana and Meritus held tight to handholds and screamed. Cleo stood there, frozen.

The black opening grew large in the forward window as though a demon were pushing us into its hungry throat.

The wing blades shook. The Silver Dare's hull vibrated. Bolts loosened, and windows rattled from roaring blasts of air.

I braced to lunge at Erikal, shouting, "It'll kill us!" But the violent turbulence slammed me to the floor. The cave surrounded us, our Sunfire light illuminating heaving, rock walls.

It was too late.

Our friend did the very thing our tribe's ancient stories said could not be done and should never be tried.

He forced us into the forbidden mouth leading to the Under-world.

6

The Wind Cave

Where are we?

I could not stop looking through the window.

As I relay this now, I wonder whether my sleep in the cab the night before had, in fact, been dreamless or if my dreams had instead been overpowered by a growing fantasy I'd awakened to.

After we'd entered the Wind Cave, I shouted to Erikal in protest, but the wind's roar drowned me out. Only Alana's screams and Meritus's hooting had risen slightly above the noise.

Those first several minutes, the Wind Cave twisted and branched, as I would have expected of a cave. This, alone, had been a sight. But Erikal was not content with that. He fought against the Underworld's howling breath. At each fork or chamber, he turned towards the passages the thundering air came from until we found ourselves in an unfamiliar world.

We rounded a final lightless corner, and the view opened up. Suddenly, the rocky, noisy cave gave way to someplace else. Although we still glided underground, it was through a cavern unlike any I could have dreamed of.

It so overwhelmed me that I disconnected from my body. Only the sight and cerebral sensations remained, and nothing else: emotions, the Equis, home. A strange impression entered my mind: that I had never before opened my eyes, and yet slipped ever deeper into an illusory state.

The raging wind had quieted when we entered the endless, smooth, and round tunnel, which had such a scale that the Silver Dare must have looked like a small dragonfly in an infinite corridor.

My four friends fell as silent as I did. The clicking of controls and my heart pounding were the only sounds. Were we all expecting to awaken?

In the grey place, my friends' bright, colorful garments of swirling geometries shouted at me for attention. What an odd thing to notice.

Erikal stood tall at the controls, assisted by Meritus. Cleo had stumbled, perhaps from shock, onto a soaked pillow next to Alana. I shuffled on the floor and sat across from them. I wanted to ask Cleo if she felt well, but the words would not come.

Cleo glanced at me. Disbelief had washed over her face as I imagined it had mine, but something else pulled at her soft features. Awe?

"I'm able to center the cab," Erikal said to Meritus, breaking the silence. "But the wings need to be set at three-quarters."

My head automatically spun towards them with the urgency of a lizard being stalked.

But then my gaze drifted to the forward view, where the cave extended perfectly straight ahead to an endless vanishing point. Every surface out there had a planar, computer-designed appearance of unvarying grey, but there were no seams or joints for the individual parts, distorting any sense of scale. Mortals couldn't create any component larger than our producers.

What magnitude of machine made this cave?

The dim light had no shadows or a visible source, giving a flat effect that worsened my ability to gauge the place's size.

But it was clearly immense. Our current height above the tunnel floor may have rivaled the seldom-seen kites, beasts who soared above the trees.

The passage evoked a circular web that we perpetually flew into. It was, however, an illusion of perspective, created by the repeating structural rings wrapping the circumference. The farther rings appeared smaller. Beams parallel to the tunnel, as well as two featureless platforms running the length of the cave on the lower right and left, completed the weblike appearance. It all seemed to draw nearer and nearer, churning my insides.

The gods created this. This is the passage to the Underworld.

I looked away, breaking the web's spell.

Erikal and Meritus must have been too focused on driving to panic. Thanks to their apparent calm, I managed to keep myself from going into hysterics. But I felt madness tapping at the glass.

"I bet we're floating so high because we're underground," Meritus said. "Floating forces come from the ground."

"Good thought," Erikal said, "but that doesn't explain why I can't do a simple slowdown . . . give me a moment." Erikal casually handled the various levers, buttons, and dials.

"Giels," Meritus shouted without turning, "hope your device is hearing all this."

Why did he say that? Because of the mortal's spirit inside it? Giels, forget why, just do something, anything. Answer. "The recorder? It should be activated." My voice sounded flat.

"Focus on driving," Alana said. "Why'd you do this, Erikal? What were you thinking?"

Good questions, Alana.

"I didn't plan to," he responded, his back still facing us. "I wanted to test the cab against the wind and go just a short way in. But, somewhere, we lost control because of the cave's power. Now the wings are functioning abnormally." He flapped a hand in the air as if portraying erratic wing blades.

Alana held the rim of the window and awkwardly squatted as though she were ready to lunge forwards to escape. "We're too high. How come we're not falling?"

"We're working on that, too," Erikal said.

"We're not working on falling," Meritus clarified, "but working on understanding why we're not falling."

Alana turned to me. "There are dead souls here. Might they enter us? That's what they do, isn't it?"

I tried to search my mind for relevant lore, but I couldn't work out the complex thought. My head felt like a poorly assembled machine shooting sparks and emitting smoke. "I'm no shaman," I said. But one fact did come to mind. My friends were more educated than most and undoubtedly knew of the beast, but I dared not remind them of the Guardian out of fear of summoning the demon.

"If there are dead souls here," Erikal said, "they didn't stop us."

Is Erikal mad? Why would he believe they let us in? And for what awful reason would they? Was he thinking they were aware of the recorder's message? My numbed body suddenly awakened, every nerve screaming.

But he was wrong. "Souls should only pass here." My voice shook hard. "Salihandron controls the cave. And it's the god's mission to stop us."

My mind is working.

"Do you recall any exact words?" Erikal asked.

"Yes," I said. "In fact, it's in a bunch of stories. Try this verse: 'To maintain the World's balance, Salihandron will see to it that, while alive, mortals could no longer return to the deep. The god forever blows its wind through the exit to keep them out...' From *Gift of the Gods*. That's it, word for word. Not much room for interpretation."

"Yet, we're here," Cleo said. "Erikal made his vehicle just a little faster and stronger than others. That actually might be why Salihandron entrusted us with the soul." Cleo had relaxed a little. She appeared apprehensive but calm.

Alana chewed a fingernail. "Then it *did* send the message. Oh, the Sun, this is more real than I imagined."

They were still wildly speculating on the recorder. But the truth that Cleo had uttered needed no discussion. It was undeniable. We were here, seeing a hidden world—us, five youths from the Deo.

"I suppose, then," I said, "we're telling a new story." That offhand statement, more prescient than I could have imagined, born of disbelief at our current situation, hinted at a simmering desire very deep within me.

The dramatic epics I recited were full of strife, war, suffering, and glory from a time before the gods sent the mortal World into its peaceable balance—a time when mortals sought autonomy, and immortals struggled to find their purposes.

Why must so much horror come before peace?

Despite their horrors, a part of me always loved the stories not so much for their history as for the way I imagined myself within their magnificence.

Cleo's eyes widened, as though something profound had occurred to her. "Our own story?" Her jaw dropped, and her eyes settled on me.

She'd found something in what I'd said that touched her.

"How do the stories describe the cave?" Alana asked.

Her question tugged uncomfortably at me. It was one I hoped to avoid. The stories talked about huge chambers, twisting passages, dripping water, darkness, and burning light in the Wind Cave and Underworld. But I couldn't recall them saying either was made up of typical caverns, as I'd always imagined. It made me feel ignorant of the truth. Seeing this place made me think our entire tribe was ignorant.

"That's it!' Erikal said. "The driving power isn't coming from everywhere, as you'd expect underground. I have a test; I'll ground-side left. Hold on! This is fantastic."

Ground-side, or "taylayk" in our language, referred to aggressive banking of the vehicle. We tilted only a little, however, and leveled off.

"I'm getting it," Erikal said to Meritus. His eyes sparkled as they often did when he discovered something new. Instead of worrying, he seemed excited. "The power must be coming from the sides only. We could probably stop anywhere."

I could only hope that was good news.

"Friends, I've just seen something," Cleo said. "It looked like an outline. A rectangle. On the wall by the walkway." She pointed towards the continuous platform on the right.

"A door," Alana said, looking through the window while clutching herself.

"Yes, actually, maybe you're right." Cleo stretched her thin neck and saddled her cheek against the glass, attempting to look back at it. "We passed so quickly, I can't say."

"Exciting!" Meritus said. "Makes perfect sense. This cave can't go on forever with no way out." Meritus had always had a keen perspective. Nothing shown to be true ever seemed unreasonable to him. He looked up at Erikal. "We've already gone far, maybe more than the Deo to the Plateau."

Could it be?

"If we had a computer," Cleo said, "we could figure out how far by counting heartbeats between each structural ring, which are maybe a hundred feet apart, and—"

"Seven hundred and fifty miles," Erikal interrupted while still handling the controls. "Which is certainly longer than the distance from the Deo to the plateau. The entire breadth of the world between the earth and sky might not be that far."

Cleo raised her eyebrows and gestured to Erikal. "I forgot. We do have a computer."

Meritus looked at the ceiling, perhaps to do the calculation in his own mind. He shook his head and turned to continue driving.

My best friends were usually confident, but their apparent comfort in our situation terrified me. They didn't seem to know the danger we were in. And nobody was taking charge. "We need to leave."

"As you implied," Erikal said to me, "we're doing something for the first time since the old stories. We'll get back, but even if we don't, can you believe that, right now, in this exact moment, we're in the Underworld? This is where we go after we die. And it seems to me, because of that, we're safe—safer than in any place imaginable."

Safe because it's where dead people live? What in the Sun did that mean?

A daunting thought came: that we might be dead and not know it. That Salihandron had not placed us on an errand but had summoned our souls with the message. Perhaps Erikal was somehow aware of the truth and now peppered us with hints. My eyes darted around as if searching for evidence. *When would we have died?*

"Giels is right," Alana said in a slow, deliberate tone. "Turn around. Take our situation seriously. The Underworld is—" She pointed through the forward windows and cried out. The cab had listed so far that we passed within feet of one of the structural ribs.

Erikal turned back to the forward view, casually pushing a lever and tapping several buttons. The Silver Dare moved from the sidewall.

"Oh, the Sun, be careful!" Alana shouted.

"We weren't in danger," Erikal said. "I knew our position."

"I wonder why there's a door," Cleo said.

"Why?" Meritus asked. "Probably so we could go through it, if we can open it."

"Meritus, as Giels will tell you, there may be some meaning—"

"Why are you talking about the door?" Alana interrupted. "Turn around, as Giels said."

Erikal again pivoted to face everyone. His eyes flashed. The flash was cold, piercing, and a little frightening. "Let's have a closer look at the door on our way back. I'd like to see if I have that much control of the vehicle."

Alana inhaled deep. "You can turn us back?"

"It's the same thing as coming out here, or should be."

"'*Should be?*'" Alana said. "And is the other option 'we travel endlessly into the depths?'" A tear rolled down her cheek. She turned to me, asking, "Is there *supposed* to be a door here?"

Our oldest stories often referenced the separation between

our world and the spirit world, and they usually included a door. Perhaps the best influence I had right now was reciting history. A passage came to mind, though it might not have added the needed urgency. I said it aloud anyway to distract myself as I held the side rail, white-knuckled:

The cave is a threshold from which all corporality flows. Love, hate, always seek one another. They are moonlit branches of two trees curling around, never touching except for the wind, a temperamental thing. It exhales strong, forever, filling or extirpating us. The threshold's door opened wide in its push. The branches swayed and broke. I closed it just enough to allow the leaves to dance.

"That's a metaphor," I said, "from the Talik Stories—*Songs of the Wind Cave.*"

"Timely," Alana said. Her body shook. "Beautiful. Erikal, I see you are excited, and I'm excited, too. I don't know. Terrified, to be honest. If you look at the door, pass it quickly."

Erikal gave a terse nod.

Far from adding to their urgency of getting us out of here, my friends' bodies seem to relax after the recitation. Even I relaxed a bit.

But it didn't last.

Turning, the vehicle jolted leftwards with a thump, as though we had been floating downstream and collided with a rock. We all cried out, except Erikal, who kept his focus. Nothing had visibly caused the impact.

The cab continued turning, thumping over and over, until we faced the direction we'd entered from. We were gliding backwards.

The ship slowed to a stop.

Underscoring how far we'd gone, the return way converged to a vanishing point, just like the outbound direction. We had travelled a distance at least matching the breadth of the World, according to Erikal.

My body leaned back with forward momentum. Thank the Sun. I cast off hovering thoughts of demons and imagined returning to the beginning of the seemingly endless passageway. We headed homebound. A sigh of relief escaped me.

As our speed increased, we descended to the left, towards the horizontal plane.

"It's there!" Alana said, pointing.

We all searched and soon saw what Alana saw. The door's surface sat flush with the surrounding wall and matched its smooth, warm-grey finish and gentle curve.

"How'd you spot that?" Meritus said.

Only a rectangular outline, a recessed handle, and a small, flush control panel on the left revealed its existence. *Why would anyone make a door so difficult to see?*

"A door, our secret door," Meritus sang. He fancied himself a Musical Orator sometimes, inventing songs.

"Um . . . I adore this door," he continued and shook his head. "I implore this door?"

You're hidden no more?

"Focus on driving!" Erikal snapped.

Seriously.

"Seriously," Alana shouted, echoing my thought.

Meritus turned to Alana, a twinkle in his eye. "C'mon. I'm always driving you. You know I have this."

Alana threw up her arms, gesturing to the forward view.

We approached the door fast.

"Stoppiiinng . . ." Meritus hummed.

We weren't stopping. I stood. "Cleo."

She sprang up to the front.

The thirty-foot-wide walking surface came at us. The cab jolted with a bang on the underside.

"I thought you had it!" I said, my back slamming against the left wall.

The ship jerked in a pivot and slid towards the precipice along the platform's edge. The left side inclined.

I grabbed a handhold to keep from slipping among screams.

Erikal and Meritus stumbled. They flew into Alana and Cleo against the opposite sidewall. The Silver Dare rolled under their weight.

The deep canyon at the bottom of the cave moved into view.

We rotated over its precipice.

After everything, it'd all end at the hands of Meritus.

7

Doors

"Fly before we fall," I shouted with my remaining hope that we could be saved. But everyone had piled against the right side, rolling the cab.

I grasped the handhold tight. But with the carpeted floor moist and at an angle, my feet slipped.

My hands scrambled to maintain hold of the handle. But I slid next to the others, further exacerbating the ship's roll towards the edge.

Screams stabbed at my ears.

A loud clang. The cab went still.

Cleo lay on top of the pile of my friends as though reposed on cushions. She stared outside. "We're actually fine! A wing blade stopped us."

My breaths heaved, and my muscles went limp.

Cleo let out a cry. "Erikal, some of the wing facets are damaged."

"Belvo damn you, Meritus," Erikal said. "You should've been reactivating the wing switches, not staring at the door, singing to it."

"It was the only thing to help calibrate our distance," Meritus said from under Alana. "You didn't put the skis down."

Erikal reached out from below Cleo to grab a handhold. "Calibrate? I didn't say we were landing and wouldn't have with the cave's power. Idiot."

Idiot? Erikal was being kind.

"You said we could *definitely* stop anywhere." Meritus poked his head up to look at me. "Right, Giels?"

I rubbed my forehead. "I believe there was a *probably* in there. No, *definitely.*"

Erikal groaned and pulled himself up, causing Cleo to slide onto Alana.

"Ow!"

Cleo rolled off of her. "Are you okay?"

Alana gave a slight nod and put a hand to her temple.

"We need to go look at the wings," Cleo said.

Meritus rose, one foot on the floor and the other on the wall. "We should test everything first." He nodded towards the controls.

"No. Cleo's right," Erikal said, "we need to verify that the wing movements match the cams while someone's at the controls. It's the only way, unless we feel like taking our chances."

Although I understood little about cab designs, I knew that the shape of each of the blade-like wing facets was essential for proper flight. If even one were in the wrong position or damaged, the cab wouldn't fly correctly, if at all.

The fall had disfigured *two* facets hanging beyond the precipice. I would ring Meritus's neck before Belvo dammed him.

"This is so awful," Alana said, her thick, wavy hair covering her face.

"Let's not assume the worst yet," Cleo said. Her voice quavered. "We might be fine."

"If not, then we're dead," Alana said, "A slow death. Starvation as we hopelessly walk our way out of this cave, if the souls allow it. Do you recall that twisting first part? Even if we made it there, how would we climb through?" Alana clawed at her scalp. Her depressing soliloquy contorted my face. But something bold and commanding came through from her. She extended her arm and finger to point firmly outside. "We don't know what's out there. Figure this out, now!"

"You're right. There could be human spirits floating about," Meritus said. "Does anyone know an incantation?" He fluttered his fingers and smiled. His attempt at humor dumbfounded me, especially when our crash was his fault.

Alana's eyes went wild at Meritus. "What a thing for *you* to say now."

"Cleo, Meritus, can you work the controls?" Erikal asked.

"Yes," they said in unison.

Meritus scratched the stubble on his thin face. "Why?"

Erikal's expression became stern, jaw clenching. "I'm going out there." He shoved a lever, which emitted a clank, indicating he had locked the wings. "I see no spirits."

"Spirits are invisible," Alana said.

"Does it matter?" Cleo said, gesturing around the interior. "Would the cab walls keep them out?"

With the ease of a spider ascending a tree, Erikal walked the inclined floor to the cab's only exit.

My nerves screamed, but I wanted to appear strong. Mental strength would be needed to get us home. I tried to match the casual attitudes of Cleo and Meritus. "It'll be windy, and you might need help. It's named the Wind Cave, after all." I intended to be glib to show confidence, but my voice shook, and the humor fell flat.

But Cleo appreciated the gesture. "Thank you, Giels."

I faked an assured smile and walked the inclined floor much less elegantly than Erikal.

Erikal, Cleo, and Meritus discussed a strategy for testing the controls. Erikal opened the door, and he and I jumped down several feet to the walking surface. The vehicle wobbled and scraped against something on the opposite side.

The air blew in a gentle, continuous flow, fast enough to exert a chill on my face and hands but much weaker than I'd expected. It carried a slight metallic odor. I braced my arms across my chest for warmth.

Erikal squatted and knocked his fist on the floor. "Metal," he said. "Very thick metal of some kind, I think. An alloy, maybe?" He remained levelheaded enough to question the makeup of the world around us.

It impressed me. Invisible beings, spirits, souls, and even deities floating about or beyond the door intruded my mind. I felt like a ramble-rodent caught in a trap, waiting, eyes wide with fear, for the arrival of the hungry trapper.

Nothing about the place was familiar, with nothing of detail to look at except the door. No wonder Meritus wanted to use it for gauging our distance.

My head spun from the cave's size and unnatural simplicity. To stave off my disorientation, I focused on the door's outline and its ominous subtlety. Had we been meant to discover it, or had it wished to remain hidden?

The parking skis shot out from the hull's bottom with a loud clang and jutted out nearly sideways. The noise reverberated.

"Come on, Giels." Erikal jerked his head to signal for me to follow him around the Silver Dare.

Our friends watched us through the forward windows. Cleo caught my eye. She smiled in the way girls do sometimes to show compassion in difficult situations. Maybe I needed to appear more self-assured. I stood taller.

A few feet of platform, not visible from inside, lay between the vehicle's hull and the precipice. On that narrow surface, we carefully moved to the wing assembly.

The outermost facets, which hung ten feet over the edge, appeared horribly bent, worse than they looked from inside. Their connecting joints and motors hung loose.

"Those are useless now," Erikal said as he smacked the wing's primary connecting strut. He waved to Meritus, who, in turn, said something to Cleo. The two adjacent, less-damaged facets moved. Meritus and Erikal continued to communicate with gestures as though they shared a secret language.

Cleo worked at the controls, but the vehicle did not lift.

Erikal pointed at the wing plate above me. "Watch those."

I shrugged, not understanding what he needed.

"Watch the motors and cam alignments," he said, and walked around to the other side.

The wing-plates moved again. They appeared functional, except for the twisted ones at the end.

"The bent cam is not moving its facet," I shouted, hoping I made sense. I guessed at which part was the cam. In my anxiety, I'd answered without considering whether my guess might endanger us further. I rubbed my face, angry with myself, but I wouldn't admit my mistake. Attempting to project confidence was honestly all I could provide at the moment.

Erikal shouted a few more commands to Meritus and Cleo. I

braced for when the vehicle would rotate away from me and onto its skis.

Will we leave? I shook from nerves. I turned homewards into the cave's impossible unending distance and imagined walking as Alana feared.

"Didn't you hear me?" Erikal said from immediately behind me, just above my ear. I jolted, nearly losing my footing, before he grabbed my arm.

"Lock the cam." He reached over my shoulder and pushed something next to a thick, curving plate. It clicked. The cab suddenly righted itself.

"Not my expertise," I said.

Erikal shouted for Cleo and Meritus to stop.

He leaned forwards, looking over the edge and shaking his head. "Amazing. This place is well beyond what I would've expected."

"Do you think we can fly?" I asked.

"Yeah, we should be fine. You know I like to be a little redundant with my designs."

A long sigh escaped me. "Good. Great. We won't have to strangle Meritus for crashing, then turn into cannibals like in *The Lost Way*." I smiled at Erikal.

"We'd die of dehydration before that," he said, not smiling back. "Anyhow, I'd jump even before dehydration hit. It's faster."

He didn't seem to catch on that I was trying to lighten the mood with my comment. Or was he trying to lighten it more by suggesting he'd leap to his death? I leaned over the ledge, holding a wing strut, and shuddered from the height, which seemed much greater standing there than when flying in the cab. "You're right, what you said about this place. It's tremendous.

Like . . ." No appropriate words came.

"Eternity," Erikal said, nodding. "Only gods could allow us to see this."

We stood next to each other, silent.

Having a moment alone with him, I asked, "Why did you do all of this? Why did we come here?"

"At a certain point, we had trouble stopping."

"No," I said. "I mean, what made you build such a powerful vehicle and decide to go into the cave at all with it."

He turned to me, raised his eyebrows, and said, "Because I could."

Because he could? The overconfident reply brought my mind to a halt.

Someone tapped on the glass. Alana.

"Let's go," Erikal said.

We returned to the interior of the now-straightened vehicle.

"How are you?" Alana asked.

"Fantastic," I said in an intentionally dry tone. Alana let out a relaxed breath. She even had a slight smile on her half-concealed lips. I didn't expect someone so nervous would enjoy sarcasm.

Erikal adjusted the controls. "We'll fly."

The others yelped with relief.

I stared through the window at the door.

"I wonder where it leads to," Cleo said, joining me. "It's automatic. Look at the controls."

"Erikal said we can fly," Alana said. "Let's not tempt this place."

"We can try the door another time, perhaps," Meritus said with a shrug, possibly to appease Alana.

But she returned the favor with scorn. Her eyes narrowed,

and her jaw dropped. "You want to return?" She stood, visibly agitated and befuddled. "We shouldn't be here and aren't even positive we can leave."

Meritus raised his palms. "Sorry, just—"

"This could be our one chance," Cleo said, looking at me. I nodded, trying not to hesitate. "Is your recorder activated?" she added and smiled, a bit of mischief coming through. "We'll certainly want to remember this."

I fumbled in my pocket and pulled it out. I thought I had activated it after Erikal played the message earlier, but it had remained off. I pressed the record button. Dropping it back in my pocket, I stared hard at the door.

Cleo touched my arm, and I turned to her. She gave me a warm, angelic smile. I had resisted every step of our adventure, from its planning to where we stood then. And yet, the girl I loved more than anyone somehow seemed to think I wanted to open the door. *How can she believe that?*

I returned the smile and nodded, and I meant the nod. Somehow, I did want to open the door. Had Cleo's misplaced confidence in me given me time to find my adventurousness? Or did something in me want to be part of this unprecedented moment? Or was it that we had done the most dangerous act by entering the cave, and yet I remained whole even after crashing?

I'd chosen to go outside, after all. And I'd leaned over the precipice.

Now I could push through and part the daunting fears before me. The feeling was unfamiliar, as though my body was numb except for the force in my heart.

The shaking and the pit in my stomach had left. I liked—no, relished—it. "Friends, outside is actually fine. The air is good, and I felt no spirits."

This strange, awful moment gave me a chance for what was certainly bravery, the hallmark of the heroes of old—an emotion that I never had much need for in the safety and certainty of the Deo.

"I'm not going out there without the spear," Meritus said. "You know, in case something's beyond the door."

"Spears? Against the souls and spirits?" Alana retorted. "Are you going mad?" She turned to me. "Giels, you should know more than anyone how dangerous this is."

"The door's the only thing our size down here. Like it's meant for mortals," I said. The recorder's weight pulled at my pocket. The realization that it was recording my bravery gave me pride.

Meritus raised his eyebrows, puckered his lips, and nodded. He seemed impressed. "Great point. If we can open it, then we open it a little, just like your Talik says."

Alana relented with a groan and looked up to the ceiling as if giving our faraway Sun a prayer.

Without a word, Cleo exited the cab and pulled me with her. Meritus and Erikal followed. Alana joined us, but she shook hard—from the crisp air or out of fear, or both—and shuffled back into the vehicle.

The four of us approached the door. Cleo slid her hand into the door's inset handle and pulled on it, but it stayed closed. We examined the control panel to the left. Nothing about it looked familiar. It had a screen of flat glass, instead of metal like our computer screens, and light, not movable etchings, created unrecognizable shapes on it. Their dim glow seemed magical. Perhaps they were.

The buttons were all grey except for a yellow and red one, and were arrayed in a seemingly useless configuration.

Cleo put her finger on the yellow button. "This one?" She

pressed it. The wall gave a whoosh, and then a click.

I jumped back.

"It's that easy," Cleo said. She pulled the handle, and the door slowly moved. It pivoted like a cab's door, but along its right side instead of at the top.

"Cleo, we're only going to open it a little," I said.

She nodded.

Meritus, who stood on my left, walked backwards. He bit his nails.

Not knowing what might be unleashed, I swallowed and joined him. The door rotated open, but only its thick edge revealed itself. The edge grew wider as Cleo pulled until, after about a foot, there came a sliver of a dark place beyond.

No odor, no light, nor beings of any sort manifested, but dread surged through my body. Meritus and I looked at each other. With widened eyes, we acknowledged each other's distress, but we did not run. We stood as still as statues, like prey attempting to go unnoticed. Perhaps fear itself escaped through the opening.

Erikal produced a small artificial light from his pocket and tossed it through the gap.

And there it was, as clear as anything in Sunlight. Although no sound, no movement, or strange beings escaped, the space beyond lit up with color.

Yellow.

Bright yellow. My growing fear now mingled with excitement. Erikal and Cleo watched as I walked to the thin opening, to a room the size of a large closet. It contained another door on its opposite side. Yellow covered every surface, but otherwise, the room was empty.

"There's nothing here," I said, "just a golden color, and

another door."

The others crowded around, creating a collective push, and the entry swung wide. We stepped into the little space. The air was warmer within.

Alana cried out from the cab and, to my surprise, ran from the Silver Dare and crammed in with us. We embraced her. In the excitement, Cleo and Erikal pulled on the handle of the second door, but it had no control panel and held tight. That door would not move, but it didn't matter. We hooted and cried out with wonderment.

The room was the color of the morning Sun, the color of hope and a new beginning—of passing a threshold. A color seldom used, even by our shaman council, because of the rarity of golden pigments in nature and the virtue of its shining radiance. The color inspired as much awe as the most precious gems.

So much yellow had the energy to power our souls.

Cleo articulated the sentiment. "It's a sign."

We all turned to the second door as though of one mind. Strange bas-relief patterns adorned it and its jambs, like our traditional stone-carved knots, but less appealing and less organized. After talking it through for a bit, we agreed the marking could be some sort of electronics or interactive shapes, like buttons. But we had no idea how to use them. Cleo touched several, but nothing happened.

Everyone looked at Erikal. It seemed natural. He had brought us here, and perhaps he knew what to do next.

"Giels," he said, "in the exterior side compartment to the left is the new do-it-all."

"Which left?"

"When facing the front."

I ran to the cab. After I opened one of the articulated curved panels on the exterior, the massive device, nearly three feet tall, floated out. Standard do-it-alls were half the size. I pushed it, sending it hovering towards the yellow room. It slowed and stopped just before the threshold.

I jogged to the device, and my friends all looked at me. Erikal was almost expressionless, as though preparing to do a routine chore. Cleo's eyes had filled with excited uncertainty. Meritus gave me a look of conspiratorial mischief. Alana shot me an unsettled sidelong glance.

It seemed we all understood what Erikal planned to do with the giant device. He wanted to destroy a door in the immortal realm. But disbelief and a desire to conform—to just go with what was happening—lessened my horror. In a way, the blatant rule-breaking excited me even though I knew nothing of the Wind Cave's rules.

But what excited me more was that the group had opened the first door and stood in that small room because I'd wanted them to.

And yet, I felt innocent. After all, I wouldn't be holding the machine.

I pushed the device towards Erikal. As soon as it entered the room, it dropped to the floor with a bang that reverberated through the cave. Alana and I both hollered in response. Meritus laughed at us.

"What does that mean?" I asked.

Erikal grabbed a handhold on the device to pull it up. It did not move. "It's almost as if, past this door, there's no lifting power."

Grunting, he used both hands, his muscles swelling under his shirt. The others looked on, mesmerized, while the device slid the width of a finger.

I straightened my thin frame and broadened my shoulders. I could have been intimidated by my friend; the feeling tried to seep in. Our predicament could have paralyzed me. But I allowed neither.

My sudden boldness had so far kept me going. I wanted to hold onto the positive feeling, just to survive the adventure, if nothing else.

"Didn't realize how heavy this thing is," Erikal said.

We both pulled the device. As soon as we dragged it halfway back over the threshold, it shot up some eighty feet and, with an enormous bang, slammed into the cave's sidewall, which rounded above like a barreled vault. The machine bounced and hovered somewhere far away in the dim light. The force of it flying up knocked me against the door jamb.

Erikal stumbled back a step and adjusted his tucked shirt. He looked up and cleared his throat. "I'd suggest we can leave it there."

"And maybe we can leave the recorder here by this door," Meritus said.

"We've come this far," Erikal said, rubbing his brow. "Let's think. It's like there's a problem here that needs solving."

Cleo placed her fingers on the unopened door. "I wish we knew whether the message in the recorder is a temptation or a command." She turned to Alana. "You believe it wanted to return through the Wind Cave."

Alana put both of her hands in her hair. "I don't know, Cleo. I imagined Erikal would toss it into the cave at the Boromount Plateau and let the gods do the rest. If we can't go further, then this is obviously not the right way."

"I agree," I said. I had forced myself to maintain confidence, but I didn't want to force my stupidity. Despite having retrieved the do-it-all, and all but encouraged Erikal to break open the door, I came to my senses and decided to use my authority of lore to herd my friends back into the cab. "The underlying theme of all our ancient stories about the Wind Cave is that curiosity kills."

"Would a god kill those who do a task for them?" Cleo said.

I could not explain the message. I could not explain our ability to descend into the cave. But I knew Salihandron did not need our help to escort a human spirit. A thought came to me that made me laugh nervously. "Cleo, that's all Salihandron does—you know, kill. He's the death-escort."

Meritus laughed as well. "Good point." He turned to Cleo. "It is a good point." She stared at him, and he straightened his face.

"You said it yourself, Giels, wisely," Cleo added. "It's as though we're part of a new story."

"Maybe," I responded. I hardly understood what I had meant, but Cleo seemed to have latched on to it. This experience, this moment, was profound. I couldn't deny that. But if we had entered our own tale, then now was probably a good ending. As Erikal had said, we'd come to a place no one had been to since the Original People had lived. No mortal could expect more than that. Nor should they want more, with what dwelled in the world below. I searched my mind for a reason to get us back into the cab.

An idea hit, something we had been saying all along. "If this is Salihandron, then we'll have no choice but to do the god's bidding. If so, then if we walk to the cab and fly home to tell the council about the message, we will either be stopped, or doing so will be the god's will." I stepped forwards, still reveling in my confidence. "This door won't open. If we're meant to be here, we'd only need to knock on the door"—I knocked—"and say hello."

With a whoosh, the door shot rightwards into the wall.

As fast as the door slid away, a thick grey cloud burst through, swirling into the little room and beyond, blinding me. "Hell!" I cried out. I sucked in air to yell again, but my lungs screamed with pain. My throat closed.

The dark, airy mass carried with it the scent of something ancient, forgotten.

My chest heaved to expel it. I strained to breathe.

Escape! I fumbled, bumped, and coughed my way out of the yellow room and back to the cave.

I ran within the horrid, expanding shroud.

"Stay to the wall!" Erikal shouted. "Don't run."

I stopped. *The ledge. Oh, the Sun.* I didn't know which way to go.

Dropping, I crawled my way, feeling for a precipice or wall as I went. I grew lightheaded. "It's drowning us!" I said through a fit of coughs.

"Evil!" Alana screamed from nearby.

The ghostly thing swirled around, a spirit come to form, coating my skin and burning my eyes.

The swirling slowed. The grey cloud thinned as it grew ever larger. Covering my mouth with my sleeve, I managed to take in short breaths. The copper and chromadium color of the Silver Dare revealed itself through the haze.

The others piled back into the cab, and I ran to them. Alana pulled me in and slammed the door shut.

Everyone coughed relentlessly. I hacked up thick, dark phlegm and spat it onto one of Cleo's pillows.

Meritus gasped for breath.

Cleo pounded him on the back, and he spat out the same black substance I had.

What in hell did I unleash?

Alana demanded that Erikal lift the cab and fly away. Instead, as if in a trance, he stood motionless, watching the formless dark entity outside drift under and around the Silver Dare.

8

Dust

"Erikal!" Alana shouted between coughs. "Go!"

"Not yet," Erikal said, his voice hoarse but calm. A couple of small coughs escaped him. "Look, it's thinning."

The dark entity crept below the cab's windows and drifted, calmly and slowly, until it reached the platform's edge. Like a fog, it slid into the lower basin of the cave.

Erikal's eyes followed it. Mine shifted between him and the creature.

"Look at that," he said and pointed. From the yellow room, light now shot out into the cave, like a Sunray in grey mist. My heart paused at the sight. I wondered if the door led to the world above, and Sunshine broke through. But no, it had a fraction of the Sun's brightness and shot out sideways, projecting a rectangle of ghostly light on the opposite wall.

I did not trust the light. I wanted to leave immediately, but Erikal's calmness fascinated me. What thoughts arose in his mind? Everyone else screamed for him to get us airborne. But, one by one, they turned from him to watch the creature or look at the bright ray.

In moments, the beast dissipated as if into the ether.

Our coughing slowly subsided.

"Are we surprised to see evil spirits?" Meritus said. "I'm guessing that was the horrid protector. What's it called, Giels?"

"The Guardian?" Uttering the name sent a shiver through me. But I was skeptical it was the demon, since our stories described the beast as more like a gross combination of creatures. Sometimes it was part boromount and human, other times, part snake and tazer. The Guardian would do much more than choke us for a moment.

The floor around the cab, especially near the yellow room, discolored as if the ghost had left an embodiment of dark memories and thoughts.

"I believe we're fine now," Erikal said. He grabbed the cab's door handle.

"Wait!" I shouted from pure instinct, but he'd already lifted the door.

Erikal jumped out and swiped his hand across the discoloration. He turned around to show us his greyed palm.

"Powder," he said. "We didn't unleash a spirit but a trap." In our language, a *trap* is a device for the capture or killing of animals for a future meal. I imagined our stunned or dead bodies lying about while our confused souls waited silently, unaware of a stalking devil nearby.

"I assume we triggered it," Erikal said, "and it's now harmless." He gestured for us to join him.

Cleo looked at me. I shook my head. "How can he know?"

"I'm going," she said.

Cleo and Meritus moved to the cab's open door. "Fine," I said. Whatever plan this place had laid for us, Cleo wanted to see it through. I couldn't allow myself to be left back in the vehicle while she did.

But survival took hold. I curled my arm around Cleo's to keep her close and behind Meritus. If she and I remained at the rear, we might escape another attack. If the others did not, she could drive us home.

Alana leaned against the back wall, pale with the fear of death. Cleo gestured for her to join us, and to my surprise, she did. She came and held my other arm.

The dust's thickness increased as we approached the yellow room, to about ankle-deep at its threshold. The yellow glowed in the light. But from the angle, I could not see the second door or what lay past it.

I leaned down and pinched the powder between my fingers. *Dust?*

"Erikal," I said, "this is not actually a powder. It's more like—"

"Dust," Erikal and Cleo said in unison. "Opening the door stirred it," Erikal added.

Cleo had her fingers over her mouth to block the dusty air. "We can tear strips off the pillow coverings and wrap them around our mouths. I used a very fine fabric."

The light both beckoned and repelled me. I decided I was in no rush, and walked back to the Silver Dare to tear up one of the pillows, being sure not to select the one I had previously spat on.

Movement caught my eye. A small cloud of dust wafted out from the yellow room. I hastened to my friends, who, except for Alana, had gone in. Lines of deep footprints ran through the open door and out of view. Their bodies blocked portions of the beaming light.

Alana and I each tied a cloth around our mouths. They worked well, perhaps helped by their dampness. I looked at her. "I'm guessing you never thought you'd be doing this when Meritus introduced you to us." A glimmer broke through her terrified eyes. My knees shook. Together we ambled, kicking up dust that swirled around our legs.

"Here's the cloth," I said as we approached.

Cleo came into view. She turned to me, her eyes sparkling. "Slowly. Come . . . take a look."

As I neared, I gained a view through the second door. A straight passageway stretched beyond, where pipes, conduits, supporting structures, and various other machinelike odds and ends loosely defined its walls and ceiling. Although from the angle, I could not see the passageway's end.

A much deeper mass of dust covered the passageway floor just beyond the second door. From immediately rising to knee height at the passageway side of the threshold, it quickly tapered down to almost nothing, where it revealed a grated surface. Dust, therefore, had piled nearly two feet high on a floor that should have prevented that very thing.

"Can you imagine—" I started, but Alana's expression of utter awe stopped me. She'd stepped forwards a couple of paces. I moved past her to get a direct view down the passage.

The path went about a dozen feet to where the pipes and other mechanical work thinned out and the floor ended. Beyond that— far beyond—a vast space glowed with the same eerie ambient light as the cave, but magnitudes brighter.

Some great distance away, a delirious amalgam of unnatural, light-grey mechanistic objects were jumbled and intertwined with one another.

An object that looked like a massive, rounded duct turned a corner, or perhaps it was an immense storage tank, tightly packed among a wall of latticework, pipes, and myriad other machinery. Judging vaguely at that moment, I estimated that single form to be as tall as a small mountain and the tubes as wide as rivers.

Next to and more extensive than the giant tank, a crag-like fissure cut at a slight angle through the wall of mechanisms. I reasoned that the opening was not some natural break but part of a disturbingly chaotic design.

The sight had the grandeur and scale of the Western Sea as we had seen it earlier. My body surged with excitement and fear. My face must have looked as enraptured as those of my friends.

Cleo, now on my left, shifted to me so that our arms pressed. As we stared, she swayed a little. The pressure and warmth of her electrified and magnified the view's intensity. I had come on the journey partly so it would be me who shared some romantic moment with her. Right then, I believed I had very much surpassed that goal.

I hope the day will end well for us.

Cleo looked at me and smiled, seemingly thrilled that I stood next to her, as though she'd decided she had been right to ask me to come on the journey, as though she had been right about me all along.

She gently touched and squeezed my hand with two of her fingers and her thumb. The unexpected gesture caused me to flinch and pull back a little, not from discomfort, but from the intensity of feeling in me.

"Is the cloth working?" she asked in a low voice. She had only wanted my attention to ask that.

"Yes. I can breathe fine."

"May I have one?"

I scoffed at myself. "Sorry, I'd become distracted." I gestured towards the view.

I noticed every minute detail of her hand touching mine—the hairs on the back of my thumb as her fingerprint moved across them—and when she let go, it was gentle. Without any of our skin brushing together, her hand left mine. I turned from the view to stare into her eyes. She glanced up, smiled, and pulled the cloths from my grasp.

Cleo moved around me, her elegant figure stepping on the dust with a light touch, her hand raised to give away the rags. Dust rested on her shoulders and hair and blackened the fabric at her ankles.

"When the air cleared, and we saw this view revealed . . ." Meritus said as he tied the cloth around his mouth. "I will never forget it. I only hope I live long, if for no other reason than that this memory can be with me."

"Giels," Erikal said, "didn't you say if Salihandron wanted us to enter through the door, we would?"

I swallowed hard. "I did say that."

"I was right all along," Alana said, astonished. "None of it seems possible, and I'm not sure I want it to be."

"Sounds like the way this works—it doesn't matter what you want," Meritus said.

Cleo again touched my arm. "Shall we take a closer look?"

"I see no reason not to," Erikal said, responding before I could. "Allow me to be in front. I'll feel the floor with one foot as we go to make sure it's solid." He turned to me. "Are you recording this?"

"Yes." Three of them had now asked about me recording the journey. Part of me preferred not to. I wondered if it was a good idea to have the device remember that I'd done the great sin of going to the world below. Another part wanted it to prove to somebody, someday, that I had.

Led by Erikal, we all stepped over the thick dust at the threshold into another world. Despite being careful, we still kicked up masses of the filth.

The damp cloth from the pillow worked reasonably well at keeping my lungs clear from the swirling grey cloud. My eyes, though, burned and watered. The whites of the others' eyes had turned red. Tears carved tendrils through the grey on their cheeks down to the tops of their masks.

Most of the dust fell through the grated floor beyond the threshold, and it swirled down below like the evil amorphous beast we thought had attacked us earlier.

Down there, multitudes of boxlike machines, ducts, panels, pipes, and other mechanical work jumbled together, and on those things sat more piles of residue, which the newly falling dust kicked up in turn. Dust puffed out in distant places after swirling through unimaginably complex spaces within the unnatural sieve. The substance tended to fall, but that did not stop the air around us from becoming dense with it.

The foul air slowly moved, tracking back towards the yellow room, clearing quickly. Perhaps it would join the wind of the cave and find its way to the world above. I turned to see it drifting into the tunnel. Alana glanced up at me, her face nearly expressionless. She had moved the hair from her large, round eyes, and they seemed to expect answers from me. I had none, and I turned back.

A short distance from where we entered, the semi-enclosed passage ended at a grated metal stair. It descended about a dwelling's height in a single run to a straight, grated path, which ran right and left.

We moved to the top of the stair. Mechanical work no longer

surrounded us, and the incomprehensible immensity of the space lay naked. All around, making up the edges of the massive place, were pipes and conduits, struts, columns, floors, mechanical boxes, and indescribable machinery, each piece simple in itself but contributing to one great machine.

Almost all of it was white, topped by grey residue. For a moment, the world spun in my eyes. I gently touched Cleo's shoulders to have a sense of where I stood. She turned and smiled, as though I'd reached for her to share our wonder. The way she looked at me made it so.

Erikal spun around, glancing at my hand on her shoulder for the briefest moment. "This is all mechwork," he said with an airy voice, using a term for the internal mechanisms that made machines function, and in which the mechanical spirits dwelled. Disbelief and astonishment filled his eyes.

Despite being mechwork, the Underworld looked unexpectedly like a landscape, as if composed of a subtle order beyond mortal understanding.

Before us lay a strange valley. In place of rocks, dirt, and trees, the landscape consisted of endless mechwork, which rose and fell like hillocks to a low point full of crevasses midway between us and the distant wall.

Unlike in a natural landscape, however, there appeared to be no solid ground. Tangled mechwork descended far below us, if not infinitely. And the other side was not defined by a river's embankment, as with a typical valley. The large tank object and massive jagged crack passage, which I described as being the size of mountains, I now saw as relatively small elements within a much broader tapestry of a great wall of mechwork that extended up and out to unbelievable proportions. I feared if I looked up and around, I might lose my balance and fall to the floor, although I looked anyway.

Above us, as far away as the sky, stretched a ceiling of the same character as the distant wall. The right and left directions of the place extended much further and ended where amalgams of structures swallowed the open air in rough, toothy pieces. Overall, that world was like a room on the scale of the gods. My head spun, and I clutched Cleo's shoulders tighter. She put a hand on mine.

Despite the unimaginable strangeness, the place felt bright and airy—more how I envisioned Heaven, not the Underworld.

"Giels?" Alana whispered from behind, as if still expecting me to explain something.

I only shook my head. The cave had not come close to my impressions of the world below, but at least it was dim and ominous. The lore never hinted at what lay before us now. We had opened a door on a great secret—in fact, two great secrets.

First, that the world below actually existed in physical form such that we did not need to be spirits to travel there, and second, that it matched nothing that I, nor certainly anyone else, had imagined.

My mind urgently worked at reshuffling reality, as though trying to right itself after having been mauled. The place confirmed what I had resisted believing since we'd entered the cave: that the sacred stories might not be right.

Despite myself, my heart lifted. I think I wanted to be scared, maybe because everything I knew told me I was supposed to be. Instead, a surge of ecstasy pummeled me from within. *It's exactly like living our own epic.*

But to what end?

"Oh, the gods! Where are we, Erikal?" Alana asked.

Erikal put a hand to his chin. "Exactly, Alana. I believe we're here."

9

We Asked You What You'd Seen

"The Underworld," Alana said from behind me. "We're in the Underworld."

I wanted to make sense of the endless machine. But I could not. Was I actually standing there? Or was it all a trick, a dream, or death?

"What a find!" Meritus said. He pushed past Erikal and trotted down a few of the steps. Grabbing a flat bar handrail as he went, he unleashed a mass of swirling dust, shielding him from our view. He appeared fearless.

"Meritus!" Alana shouted.

Moments later, a hollow sound filtered through the giant space. "Ghosts?" Alana said. "Did you hear that?"

Or demons. I scanned the vastness to see where it had come from.

"Echoes!" Meritus shouted from beyond our view. "There's something shiny to the right. C'mon."

Moments after each shout, the vast space responded with soft, indecipherable distortion—echoes with grandeur.

We walked down the stairs to the lower path. To the right

and left, the mechwork engulfed the walkway like a trail tunneling through thick hedges. And, in both directions, the walk turned after some distance, disappearing within the mechanical tangles.

Long, shiny bundles of silvery strands adorned the side of the right-hand path. Presumably, Meritus had gone to investigate those, but he was out of sight still.

Erikal took off after him. Alana and Cleo joined Erikal, but Cleo then turned and made her way back to me. "Are you waiting here?"

I pointed the opposite way. "I thought about going that direction a little, just to see."

"All right," Cleo said, her eyes beaming. "let's go."

My fingers scraped on my head so tightly that the hair pulled at my scalp. "Is this amazing or scary?" I really couldn't tell.

"I don't know. It definitely feels much less scary and more amazing, somehow. It's so open and bright, and we can see for miles and miles. Yet we actually appear to be completely alone, as though nothing has been here for many, many years. It's extraordinary, it's—"

"Not much of a hell, is it?" I said.

She chuckled and tugged at my hand before trotting ahead. Her colorful, dust-laden wrap flowed loosely from her knees to her ankles. She was the image of youthful euphoria.

Nothing cast a shadow. No corner or nook was brighter or darker than any other. Yet, somehow, all of the objects' shapes were visible because of the natural gradation of shade on their surfaces. It all gave a dreamlike sensation, like we floated down a walkway in a mechanical world of a faerie's imagination.

The air had a temperature that one does not notice. The dust reeked of age, but otherwise, breathing felt dry and clean.

After a minute's walk, side passages dotted the path to our right. We kept going, and the main walkway soon turned. There, we descended a stair. I followed Cleo and lost myself in the moment, unconcerned of danger.

The path twisted and regularly forked. We occasionally encountered more steps and full runs of stairs, always going downwards.

Cleo turned a corner in front of me.

"The Maze of Azer?" I said, referring to the mythical place at the transition between the mortal and immortal realms. Cleo did not respond. I turned the same corner—nothing, just a passage, and a stairway. I stood alone.

"Cleo," I called. After a moment, blurred echoes responded. I looked around for the way back, but the passageway forked several times behind me. I ran to the stairs. Several paths broke off to the right and left below. "Cleo?" I repeated. No answer. I ran down the stairs to the closest side pathways, but still no Cleo.

The danger of the place erupted in me as a passage from *White Cloud's Fall*.

> *On the way to the angry one, on the way to the fierce one, the Maze of Azer pulled White Cloud. He did not know the maze had been aware of him. It talked to him without words. It whispered to him without voice. The devils would lie with shouts, but the maze had no reservations about hidden deceptions.*

Three obstacles prevented mortals from descending to the land of the dead, each more fearsome than the last. First, the wind in the cave blew so hard no mortal should be able to pass. But, just in case someone was hubristic enough to push through, they would encounter the Maze of Azer, a place that confused the mind and either trapped the soul in perpetuity or led them to the third barrier. The Guardian.

How'd I forget?

My knees shook. This was the maze. It made me overlook its presence, tricking me into complacency. That must have been why the place didn't look as I thought it should. I searched for a way to run—too many options.

The dust was nearly non-existent on the pathway under the mechwork and was the same color as the grating, making tracing our steps almost impossible.

I needed to find Cleo. I pulled in a slow breath to relax.

"Cleo!" I didn't sound calm.

"I can hear you," she said from somewhere nearby. "I just went down a passage for a second."

"I nearly dropped with fright." I jogged forwards to her voice.

After a turn, the walkway exited the mechwork back into the immense open area, and as it did, a thick layer of dust covered it. About a tree's height beneath the path, the mechwork sloped away at a more forgiving angle than the steep drop near the Wind Cave.

I stepped as carefully as I could through the grey filth, but my knees shook.

What am I doing here? I pulled the recorder from my pocket. I wanted to throw it into the tangle below, as if that would relieve me from the strange world around. As if Salihandron would come, take the spirit, and possibly free us from the maze in gratitude.

What am I thinking? I was no shaman. I just memorized lore. Seeing the world around, I realized I probably could no more interpret our stories, Salihandron, and this place, than could a child. My knowledge amounted to little. My body swayed. The Underworld blurred.

"Salihandron," I whispered, "if you're here, have mercy on me."

"Giels?"

Cleo's sweet, clear voice snapped me out of my thoughts.

"Cleo?"

She stood on a walkway about a hundred yards away and a little below. I leaned over the railing to have a better look, but I stirred up more dust. Through the swirling mass, I sporadically glimpsed the most beautiful girl staring up at me.

No passage or stair connected her walkway to mine.

"Giels? Are you okay?"

"Yes. But I'm afraid—" I hesitated. I didn't want to alarm her. *But she needs to know.* "I'm afraid the maze is trying to confuse us." I couldn't stop my voice from quivering. The bravery I'd found eluded me.

Cleo screwed up her face. "What?"

Did she not know of the maze? "It might be difficult to find our way back," I clarified.

"I know," she said. She looked worried now. "Maybe we'd become carried away."

Our friends' voices reverberated in the vast space. They sounded far. I turned around. Looming over us, an enormous horizontal cylinder protruded as if resting on the slope of a mechwork mountainside. It must have been the outside shell of the Wind Cave. It gave me an idea. "That's the cave. Go back in that direction, and don't go too fast. Look for things that spark your memory. Look backwards regularly also to see what's familiar, like we do when retracing our walks in dense forest."

"Yes!" She sounded a little relieved. "And also, let's pretend like we're in the Rambles Swamp, playing the searching game, and we'll call to each other regularly."

Without hesitation, I shouted, "Boorha!" a nonsense word from a childhood game, and she replied with the correct word, "Haybewen!"

Retracing my steps, I walked within the thicket of pipes, boxes, wires, and conduits. "Haybewen!" Her shout stretched in long echoes, mixing with the echoes of our friends.

"Boorha!" I responded. Our friends' eerie, drawn-out voices tightened as though we were drawing closer.

We'll get back. After all, I couldn't know for sure how our lore applied. *Perhaps there's no danger in the maze.* I repeated the thought several times.

But the attempt at calming myself didn't work. Another sound echoed. Unlike the long and drawn-out reverberations from my friends, this had a higher, inhuman pitch, similar to the squeaking of metal on metal. It trailed off in a minor chord.

Is something here?

A chill crawled over me. I quickened my pace to find Cleo, turning corner after corner, guessing at routes that would lead to the cave.

I looked back, expecting a beast trailing behind me.

Running, I grabbed and pushed off objects to propel myself. The sound came again. Did my ears play tricks?

It's just my friends. Calm down, Giels.

"Giels!" Cleo said from nearby. "What was that?"

"I don't know," I said, nearly squealing. *What am I doing? Sound more certain.* "They're just echoes. Keep going. We're getting closer." I stopped to catch my breath. "Boorha!"

"Heybewen," she responded. "Wherever the path forks, always go to your left, and I'll go to my right. But keep heading to the cave, okay?"

"Okay."

Our voices returned stretched and thin. And within the echoes, other sounds played like ghosts.

Just the acoustics.

About fifty feet later, the passage only went right or left. I turned left. The path turned left again after several feet, and about thirty feet after that, left again. Cleo's voice no longer came from my left but the right.

"We passed each other," she said.

"I know. Stay where you are, but keep calling. I'll find you."

Focus. Don't let the maze win.

Back from where I came, I made a right. Her voice grew closer. "Boorha!" I said. After meandering seemingly in circles, I noticed a small passage on my left that I hadn't seen before. I walked down and turned a corner, and there stood Cleo.

"Giels!" she yelled. We clasped each other in a hug, and she pulled her mask down to kiss me on my temple. Our cheeks and lips brushed. She pushed at my chest with her palm, jolting me backwards, and laughed genuinely, showing all of her white teeth. The mask had kept the lower half of her face dust-free, except for the smear of our caress. "I'm so relieved," she said.

Part of me wanted to pull her in for another hug, but escape was more pressing. "We're close. I hear them messing around with the machinery."

"Was that that sound?"

"Yes, probably." She needed to focus and avoid scary thoughts.

"We're so turned around," she said. "I think all we can do

right now is go up. The mechanical work rises to the Wind Cave."

"Good idea."

Holding hands, we meandered, ascending steps towards the shell of the massive cave, occasionally catching glimpses of it.

We called out to our friends. They responded. Soon, their voices sounded as though they were beside us. And through gaps in the thick jumble of mechwork to our right, a dense mass of wavy black hair moved.

"Giels! Cleo!" Alana called.

I peered into one of the gaps. A hand scattered aside the dust on a squarish pipe a few feet into the mechwork jumble. The grey substance cleared, and Alana and Meritus's eyes showed through the gap.

"Hi there. Go that way," Meritus said, moving his eyes several times left and right. "It'll lead you back to where we started." It took us a moment to work out which way he meant. We walked down the passage and up a few steps to another path, where our friends waited.

Cleo and I ran to them, trading hugs.

Bundles of silver strands and fine chains hanging from panels adorned the right side. And beyond that, the way opened up to where the now familiar stair to the cave ascended.

We're safe. The maze had not held us with its power as the ancient stories said it would. My interpretation had been wrong. It was not the Maze of Azer. Had echoes in fact frightened me?

"Did you move any metal around, like on a hinge?" I asked the others.

"Why?" Meritus asked.

"Thought I heard that."

"These two would not stop talking and pulling at stuff," Alana said, shaking her head. "Like children."

"See, I was right," I said to Cleo. "The noises were them." *Oh, thank the Sun I was right.* My shoulders relaxed, then my entire body.

The maze had not pulled me in; Cleo and I just wanted to have fun. How could I have thought we explored it against our will?

My fear gave way to an appreciation for our safety above all else. Learning that our lore was wrong had seemed worse than the perils they described. But filled with warmth and gratitude that my body and soul remained intact, I put aside my fear. More than anything, I wanted my bed. I would try to sort out the place some other time, probably to accept that I didn't understand any of it, and let it fade like early childhood memories.

"Let's go home," I said to Erikal.

"Fair enough," he responded.

Walking to the stairs, Cleo and I swapped stories with the others, who hadn't gone far.

Meritus showed us a bundle of the silvery strands he had pulled from the panels.

Cleo touch them. "You could make jewelry with these."

"Actually, I was thinking we could—"

"Meritus," Erikal interrupted, "*I'm* thinking it is a good time to sit low and silent like hunters." He pursed his lips and nodded in a calming, fatherly way.

It put the hush into us. Had Erikal heard something? Did his ears trick him as mine had me?

On the side of the path opposite the stairs, a low wall of mechwork blocked a view of the vast open area. Only Erikal could see above the pipes.

He glanced around. Then he crouched.

"What did you see?" Alana asked.

"Shhhh," he responded.

Dust scattered around us.

"Who did that?" Meritus shouted.

"Shush," Erikal said.

"That was just me," Cleo whispered. "I hit the dust. Sorry."

I could not restrain a cough. It echoed. The others shushed me, and silence took over.

A distant sound broke the quiet, a mix of a hiss and a wail, like an ancient, angry cry. It rose with a haunting, musical quality, filling the vast space with primal power. Chills covered my body. Gasps came from my friends. Cleo clasped my hand.

The notion that we were not trapped, that this was not the maze, had calmed me, but the calm slipped. I clenched Cleo's hand tighter, probably too tight. She pulled away.

"What is it, Erikal?" Alana whispered.

With the dusty haze mostly gone, Erikal rose, his neck stretched upright. He peered over the pipes.

"What is it, Erikal?" Meritus said.

He did not respond. He stood still as a statue, his jaw going limp.

"What!" Alana whisper-screamed.

Erikal's consistently focused expression broke. His shoulders dropped. His eyes went round.

Before that moment, I never could have imagined terror on his self-assured face.

10

The Guardian

Erikal had never flinched in my presence, let alone been held unresponsive with horror in his eyes. He stood unmoving while the four of us begged him to speak.

I stood on my toes to see above the array of pipes next to the path. Cleo, Meritus, and Alana climbed up the makeshift ladder of horizontal pipes.

For a moment, I stared in denial of what I saw through a dissipating fog of dust. Or, perhaps, the creature manipulated me into a sense of innocent curiosity instead of hysterics, which would have been the sane response. Able to gaze upon it, I gained a clear, prolonged view of a demon that should have sent me running.

On the far wall of mechwork—the one that rose to the mechwork sky—hung a beast, a devil, of mind-bending magnitude. It moved between the giant fissure and the tank like a tazer feeling its way along a rock wall. Despite the distorted scale of great distance, it was undoubtedly colossal.

The creature had no fur, feathers, or scales, only leathery skin stretching tight around its bones. Flesh wings, like a tazer's, dwarfed its body despite the torso's impossible size. The wings had long, embedded fingers, but unlike a tazer, which had one hooked finger sticking out at the main wing joint, the thing had a cluster of hooked talons.

Spiked teeth extended well above the snout and below the jaw, and behind them writhed a tongue like a trapped snake. Hind legs jutted backwards from the rear, not unlike a jumping insect's, and behind them, a long, spiky tail crept its way over the machinery.

Stories could not convey such horror.

"The Sun, what is that?" Meritus said, his voice grunting and hoarse.

"There's no Sun here," Alana said, her voice flat.

The creature contorted its neck at an odd angle. It opened its mouth in a yawn so wide that the jaw appeared to disconnect from the head. Its blood-red tongue escaped the jail of fangs and slithered around its eyes.

"It's still far away," Cleo whispered. "Run."

Erikal remained fixated on the beast. "Yeah, good idea, Cleo."

Instead of running, we watched it, entranced. The creature emitted a jumble of eerie, almost magical, high-pitched sounds. It nibbled at itself with its long teeth and scratched with the talons of one of its wings.

After preening, it used its hooked talons to crawl up the mechanical wall. It turned and jumped off into the vast space between it and us.

It glided at an oblique angle to where we stood. Its wings rose and dropped the height of a small mountain in an aggressive flap. A tremendous clap of thunder rolled across the unnatural landscape. The wingbeat stopped the creature midair. It stayed in there, flapping over and over with explosive booms. Its pupilless eyes did not reveal what they scanned, but its head slowly turned until its snout faced me.

"It's seen us!" Meritus shouted.

"Hush, you," Erikal whispered. "Go back to the cave."

Before realizing it, I turned and leapt to the stairs. The others did the same. We tumbled over one another, kicking up clouds of dust. Somehow, I found myself stumbling at the rear.

Before reaching the doorway, Erikal and Cleo stopped and stared past me at the monster.

I crashed into Cleo but turned out of impulse to see the creature through the grey haze.

Its wings flapped more forcefully than before. Thunder as loud as ten lightning strikes exploded, rattling the metal and machinery around us. My knees nearly buckled. My heart pounded. Terror overwhelmed me so entirely that my mind and body froze.

It approached. Quickly. Every moment, it grew so much larger that it must've been upon me, yet it grew larger still.

Go, Giels!

Cleo had gone. I threw myself against Erikal, who still stared at the demon. He did not budge. I went limp and slid to the floor.

No one else remained outside the door except me.

"Door shut! Door shut!" someone cried.

I looked up. The door did not close. Erikal stood in the doorway, perhaps preventing its closure. He extended his hand to me.

Everything shook. My ears rang. Recovering my senses, I jumped to my feet.

The beast hung midair, creating the only shadow like a vast storm cloud. Its head turned as if towards some distant distraction. But the mechwork around the path blocked my view of what it could be.

The devil opened its mouth and emitted a high-pitched, pulsating sound—needles puncturing my ears. Pain so complete shot up my neck to my head, I expected to split open.

With another violent booming of its wings, the creature's body twisted to face the same way as its eyes.

Two white lights came into view, hitting the creature

White-hot, fiery streamers spread out from the bright projectiles' impacts. My face seared.

The monster let out another deafening wail.

I held my head to prevent it from exploding, crying out.

A machine, which I could only conceptualize as a large cab without wings, emitting blue light from its rear, streamed across my view in the same direction as the lights. Inconceivably, the vehicle was shorter than a single one of the monster's fangs.

The great beast turned away from us. Its thorny tail lashed, and wingbeats boomed. It retreated, disappearing into the faraway cavern-like fissure.

My friends' screams blended together. Only after a moment did I realize they called for me.

I started to turn but stopped. Everything blurred.

Where was I? I could have been home. No. I headed over a waterfall. Or was I by the sea? I was somewhere else.

Somewhere.

An unfamiliar voice, baritone and clear, spoke—not from nearby but from inside my mind.

"Lost souls remain in your Underworld. Stay. They cry out for you. Stay, and you'll receive some great reward."

"Giels!" Cleo shouted, and pulled at my sleeves. I turned and ran into the yellow closet.

Cleo hammered a fist into the mechanical patterns next to

the door and hollered, "Close!" With a startling swoosh, the door shut behind us. Our coughing and wheezing filled the little room.

"What was that!" Cleo shouted in the darkness.

The beast, the Guardian of the maze. I wouldn't say it aloud.

"How about that cab?" Meritus said, as though he regarded the flying machine to be as impressive as the demon.

"Giels?" Alana said. "Tell us. That thing is what we all think it is?"

I pointed at the door. "I would have thought the Maze of Azer a normal cave, like the one by the entrance of the Wind Cave." I drew a deep, strained breath to continue. I chewed my lips before uttering the beast's name. "No Guardian dwelled there, and that maze is nothing compared to what's beyond this door. The Sun—" I stopped to cough, hacking up and spitting disgusting black phlegm. "—what's out there is worthy of the greatest myths. It must be the Guardian at the threshold of the mortal and immortal realms."

Without a word, we left the yellow room. The Silver Dare sat before us slightly askew, as it had when we left. We scuttled back to it, kicking up the thin layer of dust left there before. No one cared. The grey stuff already covered our clothes, skin, and hair, which was matted down by sweat.

"Did anyone hear anything besides the beast and the cab?" I said, still heaving while I talked. I received only blank expressions.

"What did you hear?" Cleo asked.

"I—I don't know. It must have been echoes." I shook my head. I wanted to believe I'd imagined the voice or that my fear and stress had made me lose my senses.

Or could it be that, like the maze, the Guardian had tried

to trick me with a psychic attack as it did to the hero White Cloud after he escaped Azer? He survived but spent ten years wandering in seclusion, struggling to fend off the ensuing, crushing madness.

As soon as the thought arose, I repressed it.

Inside the cab, tassel-goat-fur stuffing from the pillow I had torn up floated about and clung to our sweat-laden faces and clothes.

Cleo and I sat on a stack of pillows, the torn one on top. Masses of fibers and fur mixed in with the dust in her hair. Our hands clasped tight under a mound of loose fur.

"Oh... the Sun," she said, still catching her breath.

Dayodec, the earth-mother, whose womb is the world below, stole light from the Sun to make the Underworld visible. "Yeah, perhaps," I replied. *I'm ready for the real Sunlight.*

Meritus tossed a handful of the long, jewelry-like silver strands, which he had taken from the maze, onto the floor.

As he and Erikal prepared to fly, they both let loose deafening shouts. Cleo joined them and screamed with manic relief. Alana and I looked at each other, too stunned to join in.

Stark quiet quickly replaced the excited purgations.

The drivers deactivated the cab's Sunfire lights. Only the cave's moonlike glow entered the interior.

The Silver Dare carefully rose and sped towards the world between the earth and sky. The broken wing facets hung loosely from their struts, fluttering and clanging against other parts as we went.

I must have held my breath all the way to the tight, rocky portion of the cave, where the wind howled. There, the broken facets fluttered violently.

The yellow of a Sunrise greeted us as we flew upon the

Boromount Plateau. The colors and the contrasts, the shades and shadows, stood out with impossible beauty. The sea air entered through the vents, and I drank it in.

Our short descent felt like days.

"The world between the earth and sky," Meritus said. The morning Sunlight shined the sweat and dust on his face, accentuating an expression softened by the sights.

Any momentary bravery or awe I had found in the bright Underworld had gone with the monster.

We slept or remained mostly silent while we hovered alongside the Camchaw. The damaged wings did a good enough job of carrying us in the clear weather. Erikal drove, and Cleo and Meritus again took turns helping him.

When it was Cleo's turn, I watched her and Erikal. They chatted quietly. She seemed less animated, less bright than usual. He had seduced her with this machine and enamored her with adventure. I sensed her regret. Maybe now she realized how thoughtlessly he had destroyed our dreams.

The pair floated us up the side of Ceridia while dusk approached. No one said a word.

Soon, we would come upon the first artificial lights of Deoan homes. The pit in my stomach grew heavy as I watched the world pass by. Every mile brought me closer to the consequences of my actions, including my angry parents and the disappointed council.

And madness, stoked by the Guardian?

The twilight's deep blue disappeared, giving me a slight reprieve—a sense that I could find temporary refuge in the night's darkness.

Meritus left Alana's side to drive, and Cleo, exhausted, sat beside me. Erikal looked back at her. Was that longing? I gave him a sidelong glance and caressed Cleo's hair. She sat motionless, seemingly stricken and numb.

Erikal had the arrogance to risk our lives multiple times, and perhaps risk my sanity, to bring us to the grim truth of where we go when we die, all based on Alana's delusional hunch about a message, a computer glitch. He had forced me to see a truth I wished I had not seen.

The first artificial light flickered between the trees. It reminded me that, for the next two weeks, I would spend every waking moment perfecting *The Sun and Moons*, the content of which I now struggled to square with the world below. Thanks to Erikal, the stories with the Wind Cave became puzzles or, worse, delusions.

A sudden fury rose in me. Indeed, Cleo surely felt it, too. Erikal's arrogance and the trauma it caused would impact her, and me.

What Elder Sparus had said came to mind: *Just because you feel all goes as expected, it doesn't mean that all you do is right.* Erikal had been complacent, spoiled into believing it was fine to do whatever he wanted simply because, as he'd said, he could.

I turned and whispered into Cleo's ear. "Can you believe Erikal did this?"

She smiled, giving a response like a punch to the stomach. "I know. It's all so astounding."

* * *

Meritus and Erikal stopped the Silver Dare over the garden of my home. Since my house was the furthest west, they dropped me off first.

"Giels," Cleo said as I opened the cab's door. "Is the message still there?"

Half asleep, I smiled, pretending to be chipper so as not to give away my anger. I pulled the device from my pocket. Pressing the back button several times, I managed to have it play the first words. "Can you hear me?"

"It seems it is," I said.

Cleo smiled, her enthusiasm clearly evident. "Then Salihandron's work is not done, and neither is our story."

Her words, the events, were all too much. *What did we just go through?* I turned and left without replying.

I tiptoed my way into the house, relieved that my parents had already gone to sleep. I sat on my bed. My right hand unfurled, revealing my recorder. There was something on there I wanted.

I toyed with the controls, hearing voice after voice, sometimes mine, but more often, my friends talked. It did not matter whom the device had recorded; their words sounded crisp, as though a quieter version of them sat next to me. I had the volume low.

It took me an hour to find what I was searching for—a recording of my mother and me practicing *The Sun and Moons*.

The thought that I, Giels Deo, could succumb to madness had never before seemed possible. The only way to distract myself from the idea was in my palm.

Finding the beginning of our study session, I joined my recorded self in echoing my mother, reciting sentence after perfect sentence.

Other Voices

Far, very far below the Maze of Azer, in an empty, desolate place, a young goddess sat cross-legged. She listened to the thoughts of an ancient one who occupied a space much farther below than she. The contents of the man's mind flew to her faster than time.

"You cannot allow him to stay home. Their world depends on him leaving. But understand that he will soon become important to his tribe, making your job more difficult."

Will the Guardian's psychic attack make Giels lose his mind, or will he fight to regain his legacy? What secrets are behind Giels's recorder and the message it contains? How was he able to enter the Underworld, and what does it all portend for the mortal realm?

The epic serial continues with Giels the very next day in the multi-award-winning Episode 2, Illyia.

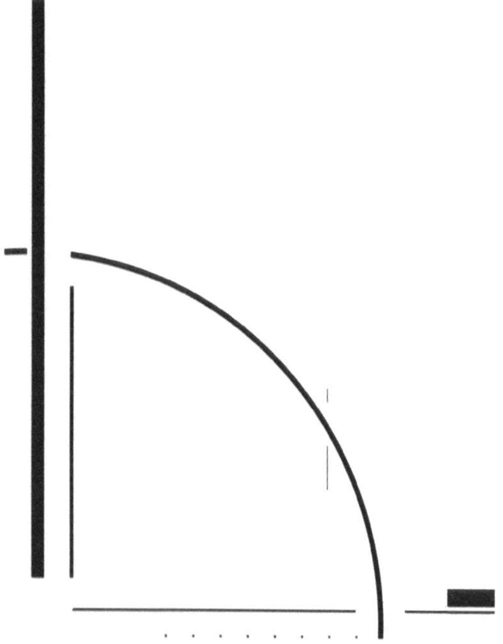